He's Out of Control . . .

"You killed my friend," Angel snapped. She made a move toward the phone on the desk. "I have to call the police."

"NO!" Darryl screamed. "You can't!"

He moved to block her.

"I have no choice. Move out of the way," Angel ordered. She tried to slip past him to reach the phone.

But Darryl shoved her roughly back.

"I won't let you, Angel!" he cried. His eyes bulged. His normally pale face darkened to red. "I'll kill you too!"

BOOKS BY R.L. STINE

Available from ARCHWAY Paperbacks

FEAR STREET
R·L·STINE

FEAR HALL:
THE BEGINNING

A Parachute Press Book

AN ARCHWAY PAPERBACK
Published by POCKET BOOKS
New York London Toronto Sydney Tokyo Singapore

AN ARCHWAY PAPERBACK *Original*

An Archway Paperback published by
POCKET BOOKS, a division of Simon & Schuster Inc.
1230 Avenue of the Americas, New York, NY 10020

Copyright © 1997 by Parachute Press, Inc.

ISBN: 0-671-00874-9

First Archway Paperback printing July 1997

10 9 8 7 6 5 4 3

FEAR STREET is a registered trademark of Parachute Press, Inc.

AN ARCHWAY PAPERBACK and colophon are registered trademarks of Simon & Schuster Inc.

Cover art by Franco Accornero

Printed in the U.S.A.

IL 7+

FEAR HALL:
THE BEGINNING

part one

Hope

chapter

1

All the books you read about Ivy State College tell you that it's a quiet, pretty school. Not a big university, but a good school, with friendly instructors and about three thousand students from all over the country.

That's what the books and pamphlets tell you.

They don't tell you about Fear Hall.

My name is Hope Mathis, and I can tell you about Fear Hall—because I live there.

Fear Hall is the biggest student dormitory at Ivy State. It's a tall, redbrick building. Sort of old-fashioned looking, with a thick carpet of ivy running down the sides, curling into some of the windows.

I'd guess that maybe fifty girls live in the rooms on my floor, the thirteenth floor. Fear Hall is only a block from The Triangle. That's the big, grassy area in the middle of campus.

But even though our dorm is so close to the center of the campus, it's only half full.

Know why?

Because of its bad reputation.

As soon as I moved my stuff into my room—13-B—in September, the other girls started telling me stories about Fear Hall. Frightening stories.

They told me that the dorm was named after Duncan Fear. He donated the money to have it built. He's a guy from a rich family that lives in Shadyside. That's a town about fifty miles from here.

The Fear family is supposed to be unlucky, or evil, or something. And I guess a lot of unlucky and weird things have happened in my dorm.

I don't mean strange sounds at night. Creaking doors. Stuff like that.

I mean things like girls seeing ghosts. And strange creatures floating through the halls. And kids disappearing and never being seen again.

I'm not sure if I believe any of the stories.

But the campus store sells T-shirts and sweatshirts that say: I SURVIVED FEAR HALL.

Sure, it's a joke. But a lot of kids at Ivy State don't think it's funny. And I think that all the jokes and weird stories are the reason why the dorm is only half full.

Some floors are totally empty. But my little room on the thirteenth floor is crowded enough.

THE BEGINNING

I have three roommates—Angel, Eden, and Jasmine.

We're all freshmen. We've only been here a month. But we're really close friends. We're like a family. Because we all knew each other in high school.

It's a good thing we're so close. Because the four of us are squeezed into a room that's barely big enough for one!

Should I describe my roommates?

Well, maybe I should start with me. I'm about five seven. Not too tall, not too short. I have blond hair—long and straight, because I don't like to spend a lot of time on it.

I have light brown eyes and an okay face. I think it's a little too round. And I think my eyes are too close to my nose.

I guess I could lose a few pounds. Maybe more than a few. But I don't mind being a little chubby.

Whatever. I'm not the kind of girl who spends a lot of time gazing into mirrors.

At least I don't spend all my time worrying about every bite of food the way Angel does. Angel is skinny and blond and very hot looking. The guys all go nuts for her.

She has a soft, little voice that sounds more like purring. The guys all think that's really sexy. And she slinks around in tights and midriff tops, even though it's fall.

My other roommate, Eden, is sort of the opposite of Angel. She's kind of plain and grungy. You know. She wears a lot of big sweaters and sweatshirts over baggy chinos. Lots of flannel shirts from L.L. Bean. No makeup at all. She has light brown hair, very curly, that just bounces around on her head.

Eden has a hoarse, scratchy voice. She's kind of loud. She says whatever is on her mind. And she's always cracking jokes.

Eden writes to her mother. Just about every night. They seem to have a really close relationship—not like me and my mom.

Unlike Angel, she doesn't seem at all interested in the boys here at Ivy State. I've never even seen her *talking* to a boy.

Eden calls Angel "Miss *Purrr*fect." I don't think Angel likes it. But she and Eden get along okay—for opposites.

Jasmine is the quiet one. I've known her for three years. And I've been living with her in this tiny room since September, and I can barely tell you a thing about her.

She's very shy. It's almost impossible to get her to talk about herself. I think she grew up somewhere out west. But I'm not sure.

She's very pretty. She has bright green eyes that crinkle up when she smiles. She has a great smile that shows off all her teeth. And she has wavy, straw-colored hair that falls perfectly down past her shoulders.

But Jasmine is so shy and self-conscious, I don't think she knows how pretty she is. She doesn't go out much. She's the brain of our group. Always has her face in a book.

She's taking some really hard courses. Advanced

courses. Jasmine thinks she might want to go into pre-med. But she isn't sure she's smart enough.

Believe me—she's smart enough. If we could only find a way to build up her confidence!

Anyway, that's our little group. The four friends of 13-B.

We're all very different. But we were really happy.

Until the night the trouble started.

That night, everything changed.

I'll never forget being awakened that night. Hands shook me roughly.

Still half asleep, I opened my eyes. Squinted up in the darkness.

My eyes stopped at my clock radio. Nearly one in the morning.

The hands shook me again. I sat up in my bed.

"Darryl—what are you doing here?" I whispered. My throat was clogged from sleep.

Darryl is my boyfriend. He leaned close. His hands still gripped my shoulders. I could smell beer on his breath.

I glanced around to see if he had awakened my three roommates. No.

"Darryl—" I whispered. "Get back to your room. You know boys aren't allowed on the girls' floors after ten."

He didn't move. His hands tightened on my shoulders. Even in the dim, gray light from the window, I could see the fear on his face.

"What are you doing in here?" I repeated.

"Hope, I'm in big trouble," he said.

chapter

2

I sat up and squirmed out from under his hands. I swallowed hard. "Trouble?" My mouth felt so dry. My breath was sour from sleep.

He nodded and took a step back. A hoarse cry escaped his throat.

"You've got to help me," he said, his voice cracking.

I raised a finger to my lips. "Shhhh. You'll wake up Angel, Eden, and Jasmine."

He stared blankly at me. As if he didn't understand my words. "I don't care who I wake up," he said finally. "I mean—I'm in trouble, Hope. I—I did something terrible."

I felt a chill roll down my back. The skin on my arms prickled.

THE BEGINNING

I stood up and pulled down the long, white cotton nightshirt I was wearing.

I pushed back my hair. The room was cold. But I felt drops of sweat on my forehead. "What did you do?" I demanded in a hoarse whisper.

His pale blue eyes flashed, gray in the dim light. His mouth opened and closed. No sound came out.

He shook his head. His longish hair fell over his face. He swept it back behind the shoulders of his leather bomber jacket. "I followed you," he confessed. "I followed you tonight. I saw you out with that guy Brendan."

I gasped. "But that wasn't me!" I protested. "I didn't go out with Brendan. Angel did."

Darryl grabbed me. His fingers tightened around my arms. "Don't lie to me!" he shrieked. "I *saw* you!"

"Let go," I whispered. "Please, Darryl—"

He has a terrible temper. Sometimes he really scares me.

One second he'll be perfectly in control. The next second he'll be in a screaming rage. A total lunatic.

He can also be very understanding. Very kind.

I met Darryl back in high school. He rescued me. From a guy named Mark.

But that's a very long story.

I was so glad that Darryl decided to come to Ivy State. It's been awesome to have him here with me. He and my three roommates have really helped me make the big jump from high school to life at college.

If only he weren't so jealous. So possessive.

He never wants any other guy to *look* at me!

At first, I was flattered. I mean, no boy ever cared about me that much before.

But when I saw how jealous Darryl became . . . when I saw his temper rage out of control . . . I knew I'd have to be careful.

I knew that Darryl could be someone to fear.

"Darryl—let go," I pleaded. "That wasn't me you saw with Brendan. It was Angel. I swear."

He let out a sigh. His hands loosened their grip on my arms. "I—I did something terrible," he stammered.

"What?" I demanded. "What did you do?"

His pale eyes locked on mine. "I carved him, Hope," Darryl whispered. "I carved him."

chapter
3

I couldn't help myself. I let out a scream. And sank back onto my bed, my head spinning.

I heard stirring around the room. Eden groaned. "What's going on?"

"Who screamed?" Angel cried.

The ceiling lights flashed on. All three of my roommates uttered startled gasps when they saw Darryl standing over me.

"You're not allowed in here!" Eden shouted. She pulled her blankets up to her chin.

Jasmine gaped at him silently, her blond hair tangled around her face.

"Darryl, what's your problem?" Angel asked softly. She jumped to her feet. "Why did Hope scream?"

Darryl spun around, his mouth open. Now everyone could see the fear on his face.

Eden shrank back. Jasmine eyed him suspiciously. Angel crossed her arms in front of her pajama shirt and stared hard at him.

"Darryl thought he saw me out tonight with Brendan," I explained. "He thought—"

"But *I* was out with Brendan!" Angel protested. "I was wearing Hope's red outfit. You're so weird, Darryl. How could you think—"

Darryl's angry stare silenced her.

"I think I killed him," he murmured.

"Noooo!" Eden shrieked, pressing her hands to her face.

"You're kidding—right?" Angel whispered hopefully.

Darryl's expression showed all of us that he wasn't kidding.

"You've got to help me," Darryl pleaded, turning back to me. "I'm pretty sure I killed him. I carved him really bad. I just lost it."

He sighed. "You know how I get sometimes, Hope."

I gazed past Darryl. Eden had covered her face with both hands. I could see Jasmine trembling from across the room. Her chin quivered. She was about to burst into tears.

Angel stood perfectly still, her arms crossed in front of her. She chewed her bottom lip and stared hard at Darryl.

"We can't help you," Angel said finally. "What do you expect us to do? Hide you under the bed?"

"You've *got* to help me!" Darryl exploded. He tore off the leather jacket and heaved it against the wall. "I—I think someone may have seen me. I'm not sure. I panicked and ran up here."

His pale eyes pleaded with me. "I didn't know where else to go," he added softly.

"Darryl, we can't do anything," Eden insisted, lowering her hands from her face. Her eyes were red and wet.

"You killed my friend," Angel snapped. She made a move toward the phone on the desk. "We have to call the police."

"No!" he screamed. "You can't!"

He moved to block her.

"We have no choice," Eden insisted.

"Move out of the way," Angel ordered. She tried to slip past him to reach the phone.

But he shoved her roughly back.

"I won't let you, Angel!" he cried. His eyes bulged. His normally pale face darkened to red. "I'll kill you too!"

Angel opened her mouth to scream.

A hard knock on the door made us all turn.

The police!

chapter

4

I froze.

My heart stopped.

I saw a flash of white light. I really felt as if I'd stopped breathing.

Another round of hard raps on the door set me into motion. I took a deep breath—and shoved Darryl toward the clothes closet. "Quick—get in!" I ordered.

He stumbled over a pile of dirty clothes in the center of the floor. Then fumbled open the closet door and slipped inside.

I spun back to the door.

How did the police get here so quickly? I wondered. How did they know that Darryl was hiding in my room?

Another series of hard knocks.

"Who is it?" I called breathlessly.

"It's me—Melanie," a voice called.

One of the nosy girls from 13-A across the hall. The three M's—Melanie, Mary, and Margie.

I really can't stand any of them.

All three of them are so smug and superior. Real preppies. I mean, the worst kind. They all went to fancy, private high schools. And they really turn their noses up at public school kids like me and my roommates.

I've had a few unpleasant run-ins with Melanie. A few weeks ago, there was a mix-up with the laundry. Somehow she thought I stole a silk sweater of hers.

It was all a big mistake. But she was so nasty about it.

Like I really need her ugly, preppie J. Crew sweater.

We're all supposed to be friends in this dorm. I mean, where does she come off accusing me of being a thief?

She and her roommate Mary are both on the swim team. And they strut around with their sleek, perfect bodies. As if they're great white sharks and the rest of us are guppies or something.

It's really disturbing.

I hate them. I really do. Especially Melanie.

And now here she was, pounding on my door in the middle of the night, snooping as usual.

I checked to make sure the closet door was closed with Darryl behind it. Then I pulled open the door to the room.

"Is everything okay?" Melanie asked. She stood

there in her silky, green bathrobe, looking perfect as always—even at one o'clock in the morning.

She has short, straight brown hair with bangs across her forehead. And the bangs were even perfectly straight! Under the shiny robe, I could see how broad and powerful her shoulders were from all that swimming.

"Yeah. No problem," I replied curtly. She knows I don't like her. Why try to hide it?

"I heard a lot of noise," Melanie said, peering over me into the room.

I knew she wanted to come in. So I stood in the center of the doorway, blocking her path.

"It woke us up," she added, motioning with her head to her room across the dark-carpeted hall. "I thought maybe you were having some sort of problem."

She kept trying to see over me. I deliberately stayed in her way.

"Sorry if we woke you," I said. "It was just our usual late-night gabfest."

She narrowed her eyes at me. Studied me.

"Sometimes we start laughing and goofing on each other, and we forget how late it is," I added. I smiled and shrugged. "Sorry about that."

Melanie continued to stare hard at me. As if she were trying to see in my eyes if I was telling the truth or not.

I lowered my gaze to the floor.

"You . . . uh . . . really don't need help?" she asked softly.

I shook my head.

I wondered if Darryl had enough air in that closet. It's a really tiny closet, and it's jammed full of our clothes.

I wondered what he was thinking about in there. I never saw him more frightened or more out of control.

I shuddered.

Poor Darryl. So jealous all the time. Maybe he cared about me too much.

"Well, I just thought I'd check," Melanie said. "Mary isn't back yet. But Margie and I were a little frightened. I mean, we heard a commotion in here, and . . ." Her voice trailed off.

I just stared back at her.

She backed up. "Well, good night, Hope."

I started to say good night.

But I was interrupted by a shrill scream of horror.

chapter

5

It sounded like the wail of an injured animal. It echoed down the long dorm corridor.

"Huh?" Melanie let out a gasp.

I gripped the door frame—as Mary burst around the corner of the hall.

"Help!" she shrieked. "Oh, please—somebody help!"

Melanie dove toward her. "Mary—what is it?"

"Murder!" Mary shrieked. "A boy—he's been *murdered!*"

Doors flew open.

The hall filled with frightened cries. Confused voices.

"He's outside!" Mary wailed. "The boy! He's—he's been *cut to pieces!*"

Before I realized what was happening, I was running along with everyone else. Running to the elevator. Running to the front doors of Fear Hall.

Like a wild stampede of cattle.

All of us in our nightshirts and pajamas and bathrobes. Our hair flying around our heads. Crying. Shouting.

I never heard a sound like it.

I never felt so excited and upset and terrified—all at once.

We pushed out through the front doors. Into the crisp October night. The ground hard. The grass shimmering under a silvery frost. A pale sliver of a moon hanging low over the campus trees. The ivy up the walls shivering in the wind.

Bare feet thudding on the pavement. A stampede of bare feet.

Running around the side of the dorm. Leaves blowing over our feet.

Running to the row of low bushes that lined the side of Fear Hall.

And there he was, sprawled over a bush, on his stomach, arms outstretched as if hugging the bush. There was the body.

Or what was left of it.

Cut up. All cut up. All slashed and torn and cut up.

Cut up. Cut up.

"I *know* him!" Mary shrieked. Her hands tugged at the sides of her curly red hair. "Oh *noooo!* I know him!"

"It's Brendan!" Melanie gasped.

Frightened cries rang out. Shrieks and gasps.

I saw a girl spin away, sickened by the sight. At the corner of the building, another girl dropped to her knees and vomited noisily onto the grass.

I heard the high wail of sirens in the distance. Shouts and cries all around. So loud. So terrifying.

I pressed my hands against my ears.

And gazed again at Brendan. His ripped body spread over the bush. Hugging it. Hugging it.

A last hug.

When I turned away, gasping for air, I found Melanie staring at me.

"What?" I demanded sharply.

She squinted harder at me. "Hope, didn't you go out with Brendan tonight?"

"Excuse me?" I cried angrily. "Have you been *spying* on me?"

Melanie's mouth dropped open. "Spying? Of course not. Why would I spy on you?"

She turned to Brendan's body, made a disgusted face, then quickly turned back to me. "It's just that I thought I saw you and Brendan walking across The Triangle after dinner."

"No. It wasn't me," I replied coldly. "Maybe you should get your eyes checked, Melanie."

She swallowed hard. Mary was beside her, trembling and crying her eyes out.

"I knew him. I *knew* him," Mary kept murmuring. "I can't believe it. Someone I know . . . someone I *knew* . . . has been *murdered!*"

Melanie slipped her arm around Mary's trembling

shoulders. I watched her guide Mary back into the dorm.

The sirens grew louder.

Girls were crying. Covering their eyes. Comforting each other.

I thought of Darryl. I wondered if he was still hiding in our clothes closet.

I suddenly had the urge to shut everyone up. I wanted to stand in front of them and shout: *"It was all a mistake! It's just a mistake! Darryl thought it was me—but it was really Angel!"*

But, of course, that wouldn't help poor Brendan, would it? It was too late to help Brendan.

I shivered. And realized I was half frozen, standing out there in the cold in my nightshirt and bare feet.

Turning away from Brendan's cut-up body, I wrapped my arms around myself and hurried back into the warmth of the dorm. As I stepped inside the lobby, I saw flashing red lights reflected in the glass door. I glanced behind me to see two ambulances screeching to a stop in front of the building.

"Too late for them," I murmured to myself.

I took the elevator to thirteen and hurried to my room, still hugging myself, still trying to warm up.

I found Darryl sitting on my bed, hunched over glumly, head resting in his hands.

I closed the door carefully behind me and stormed up to him. "How could you do that?" I demanded. "How *could* you? Are you crazy?"

He didn't look up. "Maybe," he muttered.

"Maybe?" I cried shrilly. *"Maybe* you're crazy? Do

21

you think it's *normal* to slice up a nice guy, a guy we all know?"

"Maybe I *am* crazy," Darryl repeated softly. Then he pulled his head up from his hands and narrowed his eyes menacingly at me.

"I'm warning you, Hope," he said through clenched teeth. "Maybe I'm real crazy. But I'm giving you fair warning. Don't do it again. Don't go out with another guy."

"But—but—" I sputtered. "I *told* you—it wasn't me. It was Angel."

He jumped to his feet. Nearly knocked me over. His pale eyes burned into mine. "Just don't go out with another guy," he warned. "Or I might do it again. I just might."

He staggered out the door before I could say a word.

Less than a minute later, someone pounded hard on the door.

"Who is it?" I called. "Melanie? Are you back again?"

"Police," came a deep-voiced reply. "We need to ask some questions."

I turned to Angel. "You'd better answer it," I told her. "They'll want to talk to you."

I watched her pull open the door. But I was thinking about Darryl. Thinking hard.

What was I going to do with him?

part two

Jasmine

chapter
6

"A little more coffee, Jasmine." Mrs. Jacklin raised her cup and shoved it into my face.

I set down the rag I'd been using to wipe the counter. Then I dried my hands on my waitress apron. And filled the old woman's cup from the pot that had been simmering on the burner since the morning.

Mrs. Jacklin comes into Campus Corner every afternoon for coffee and a sweet roll. She used to teach at Ivy State. History courses. She likes to tell me stories about what the campus was like in the old days.

But I seldom have time to listen. Campus Corner gets pretty busy in the late afternoon. It's one of the most popular coffee shops on campus.

And since I'm the only waitress on duty from four to seven, the job really keeps me hopping. Marty Dell, the owner and grill cook, keeps a close eye on me from the kitchen. He never lets me goof off for a second. I think he keeps track of every glass of water I take!

But I don't complain. I'm lucky to have the job. It pays just enough to keep me going from week to week. To pay for textbooks and other school supplies. And, once in a while, I can even buy something new to wear.

So I put up with Marty, the slave driver. I work as hard as I can. And I don't protest or say anything back when he's always on my case.

I think the job is even helping me with my shyness. It forces me to talk to people. I have to go up to them and smile and make conversation. Which I'm not good at.

My mother always called me Fish.

Isn't that a disgusting nickname? She called me that because she said I had the personality of a fish. A dead fish.

My mother wasn't very kind to me. She never did anything to build up my confidence. Instead, she always tried to tear me down.

I've always hated being shy. I never could understand what was different about me, what was lacking in me.

Why could other kids laugh and joke with each other, while I just stood there feeling embarrassed? Why couldn't I just walk up to a group of kids and start a conversation, the way others did?

Today I understand that some people are naturally shy.

But it doesn't really help to understand. It doesn't make me feel any better about myself.

I'd rather be like Angel. So free and easy with people. Angel can talk to anyone. And she's so amazing with boys!

She starts purring at them in that whispery voice of hers. And they don't care *what* she's saying! It's almost as if Angel hypnotizes them.

What incredible power!

Sometimes I borrow her sexy clothes. Her midriff tops and little skirts and tights. I try to purr the way she does, talking really slow and soft. And I try her slinky, catlike walk.

But it only makes me feel uncomfortable. And silly.

I'll always be Jasmine, I tell myself. I'll never be Angel. So I have to find a way to be the best Jasmine I can be.

Which is one reason why I keep my waitress job.

Angel and Hope are very understanding. They accept me being shy and not talking much.

Eden laughs at me and cracks a lot of jokes at my expense. But that's just her way.

I'm lucky that I like my roommates so much. I feel really close to all of them.

"Just a splash more coffee, Jasmine." Mrs. Jacklin held up her white coffee cup again. Her hands were so old-looking, red and splotchy.

The red made me think of Brendan.

Brendan. And blood. Brendan's blood.

Anytime I see anything bright red now, I think of that poor guy. I see his body slashed and torn, as if a wild animal had ripped him apart.

He was murdered two days ago, and I haven't been able to stop thinking about it.

None of us has.

And just as I thought of him, I heard someone say his name.

I poured the coffee for Mrs. Jacklin. I had to tip the glass coffeepot all the way because it was almost empty. As I finished, my eyes went to the booth against the wall.

And I saw the three M's: Melanie, Mary, and Margie—the girls who live across the hall. They were leaning over their menus, heads close together, expressions somber. And they were talking about Brendan.

Talking in low voices.

And every few seconds they looked up—*at me!*

Hey, what's the story here? I wondered.

Why are they staring at *me?*

chapter
_____

7

At first I thought maybe I had a stain or something on my waitress uniform. Or maybe my hair was messed up.

That's the way I think. I'm so self-conscious.

I heard Mary say she's had nightmares every night. She shook her head and her curly, red hair shook with it.

And then Melanie said she hadn't been able to concentrate on her classes at all. She tugged at the long, dangling silver earring she always wore.

Margie didn't say anything. But she kept glancing up at me, like the others.

"Brendan was a great guy," Melanie said. She tapped her long, perfect red fingernails on the plastic menu.

29

Red fingernails. Red as blood.

Why did they keep looking at me?

"I can't believe someone killed him right outside our dorm," Margie said in that squeaky mouse voice of hers. She looks a lot like a mouse. Her turned-up little nose even twitches like a mouse nose.

"Fear Hall," Mary murmured. "I always thought the scary stories were a joke."

"Some joke." Margie sighed.

They all glanced up at me again.

I pulled out my pad and walked over to their table. I heard the jingle of change on the counter behind me. Mrs. Jacklin was leaving me my usual thirty-five-cent tip.

"Why do you keep staring at me?"

I didn't mean to say that. I meant to say, "What can I bring you?" But the words fell right out of my mouth.

"Why do you keep staring at me?"

Margie opened her mouth in surprise. I could see that she didn't expect me to ask that.

But Melanie had an answer, as always. "We . . . we just wanted you to come take our order," she told me, blushing. She tugged tensely at her long earring.

I raised the pad and pulled the pencil from my apron pocket. Mary and Margie ordered plates of French fries and Cokes. Melanie ordered a tossed salad and a Diet Coke. Typical.

I could see Marty watching me through the open window to the kitchen. I knew if I spent too long chatting with them, he would flash me an angry look.

I handed their order to Marty and slid the thirty-five cents from Mrs. Jacklin off the countertop and into my apron pocket. Every little bit helped.

"Hi!" I called out to Eden and Angel as they slid into the booth across the restaurant from the three M's.

I put on a fresh pot of coffee. Then I untied my apron and pulled it off. I hung it on the hook on the kitchen door. "I'm taking a ten-minute break," I told Marty.

He looked at his watch. Every day I take a ten-minute break at five-thirty. And every day Marty looks at his watch.

I made Eden slide against the wall, and I dropped into the booth beside her. "What's up?" I asked them.

They both shook their heads glumly.

I felt a stab of fear in my chest. "What's wrong?" I asked.

"It's Hope," Eden murmured.

"Huh?" I gasped. "Has something happened to Hope?"

chapter

8

"No. Hope is okay," Angel replied softly. "It's just . . . we're worried about her."

"And Darryl," Eden added, frowning.

Angel pulled a piece of lint off her white sweater with her purple fingernails. Her lipstick matched her nails. She had two purple earrings in each ear.

Angel thinks a *lot* about how she looks.

"Hope is just so crazy about Darryl, she won't listen to reason," Angel complained.

Eden nodded. "Darryl is a total creep," she said. "He's a psycho. A real nut case. He should be locked up."

I pictured Brendan once again, sprawled over the bush beside the dorm.

"You're right," I told Eden. "Darryl *should* be locked up."

"He's dangerous. He should be put away—before he hurts someone else," Eden replied.

"Before he *kills* someone else," Angel said, her eyes wide with fright.

"But Hope won't listen to us," Eden told me. "Hope wouldn't let us tell the police. She won't let us turn Darryl in."

"It's because of what happened in high school," Angel added. "It's because of how Darryl helped her in high school."

"No. It's because she's so crazy about him," Eden argued. "But Hope is making a big mistake by hiding him, by protecting him. A *big* mistake."

I nodded in agreement. I didn't know what else to say. It was three of us against one of Hope.

"Maybe if all three of us talk to her . . ." I started.

Angel shook her head. "She won't listen. I know she won't. She has her mind made up. She's going to protect him."

"But doesn't that make us accessories?" I asked.

They raised their eyes to me. "Accessories?"

"Yes," I said. "Can't we get in major trouble for helping a murderer? For not telling the police what we know? Isn't that a serious crime?"

"We've got to talk to Hope," Eden said firmly. "As soon as we get back to the room."

I glanced up. Across the restaurant, the three M's were all staring hard at us. They had stopped talking. They were staring at us in silence.

33

"Jasmine—?"

Marty's voice made me turn to the kitchen. I found him staring at me too. He had the oddest expression on his face.

"Jasmine—are you okay?" he asked.

"Yeah. Fine," I called to him.

I leaned across the table to my two friends. And I whispered, "You guys had better go. You're going to make me lose my job."

I didn't leave the restaurant until about seven-twenty. The dishwasher was broken. And Marty made me wash all the cups and glasses by hand.

I didn't really mind. He always paid me overtime when I worked late.

But I couldn't understand why he kept staring at me all afternoon. Studying me. Like I was a bug under a rock or something.

A couple of times, I started to ask him what his problem was. But each time, I chickened out.

Jasmine, don't look for trouble.

That's what I told myself.

I dried my hands and hung up the towel. Then I picked up my backpack from the supply closet and headed to the back door.

Marty locks the front door at seven. So I always leave by the back.

"Are you working tomorrow?" he asked as I stepped out into the alley.

He knows the schedule. He knows that I work four

afternoons a week. But he always has to ask if I'm working tomorrow.

I nodded. "Yes. See you tomorrow."

"Going to meet friends?" he asked. Why was he staring at me like that?

"I'm heading back to the dorm," I told him. I turned and took a few steps into the narrow alley.

When Marty closed the restaurant door, I was left in total darkness. There were no lights back there.

The solid back walls of brick buildings on one side. A tall wooden fence on the other.

A cold wind blew through the alley, ruffling my hair, pushing me back. I leaned into it and tried to walk.

This alley always gives me the creeps. The other night, a huge rat jumped from a garbage Dumpster and scurried right over my shoes.

I only have to walk half a block through the dark alley. Then it opens onto Pine Street, which leads to the dorm two blocks to the north.

I was nearly to Pine Street when I heard the crash of a metal garbage can lid behind me.

The sound startled me, making me jump.

I didn't turn back. I was sure the gusting wind had blown the lid off the can.

I was sure—until I heard the thud of footsteps on the alley pavement.

Then I knew that someone was running after me.

I spun around and squinted into the blackness. "Marty—is that you?"

Did I forget something in the restaurant? Was Marty bringing it to me?

"Marty—?"

My voice caught in my throat.

If only I could see.

"Marty?"

The footsteps pounded the concrete alley floor.

Then two hands grabbed me. Grabbed me hard around the shoulders.

The hands slid down to my waist. Started to pull me against the building wall.

And I opened my mouth to scream.

chapter

9

*B*efore I could utter a sound, a hand clamped down hard over my mouth.

I let out a terrified grunt. Tried to bite the hand. But it pressed tighter against my face.

Choking me. Smothering me.

I struggled to squirm away.

But the other hand shoved me against the rough bricks of the wall.

A face pressed up against mine.

A young man.

I smelled peppermint on his breath. I smelled sweat.

And then I saw his face.

Darryl.

I raised both hands and shoved him back. An angry

cry escaped my throat. "Darryl!" I gasped. "Let go of me! What do you think you're doing?"

A car rolled by up ahead of us on Pine Street. A pale glare of yellow from the headlights washed over the building, washed over us.

Darryl's blue eyes stared into mine. Beneath his leather jacket, his chest heaved up and down. He breathed noisily. His face so close to mine. I smelled the peppermint again.

"Jasmine—" His voice escaped in a choked whisper. "Are you going to turn me in?"

"Huh? Me?" I cried. I swallowed hard. My waist ached from where he had grabbed me.

"Are you?" he demanded. His face slid back into darkness. "Are you and your roommates going to tell the police?"

I sucked in a deep breath. How should I answer?

"No," I told him. I lowered my gaze to the ground. "No. We're not going to tell anyone."

His face moved in and out of the pale light from the street. He didn't blink. His eyes were locked on mine. His upper lip twitched.

Nothing else moved.

Time didn't move.

"Really," I insisted. "No lie. We're not going to tell, Darryl." If only my voice didn't tremble like that.

Did it sound to him as if I were lying?

His face didn't give him away. He still didn't blink. His expression was a blank. As if he were no longer in there.

His lip twitched again.

"Okay," he said finally. He sighed and wiped the sweat off his forehead with the sleeve of his jacket. "Okay."

"But you should get help," I told him.

I shut my eyes. Had I said the wrong thing? Was he going to explode now? Was he going to hurt me?

He grunted. His body relaxed. He loosened his fists, let his hands drop to his sides.

I took a breath. "You have to get your temper under control," I said softly.

Darryl nodded. He still hadn't blinked. "I'm working on it," he said.

"Can I leave now?" I asked timidly.

His pale eyes shimmered in the dim light. "Hey, Jasmine?"

"What?" I asked impatiently.

"I promise."

"Promise what?"

"I promise I won't kill again," he told me.

Then he gripped my wrist and squeezed it really hard. And whispered, "Unless I have to."

part three

Eden

chapter

10

"*E*den, what are you doing?" Hope called to me from across the dorm room.

"Knitting a pair of socks. What does it *look* like I'm doing?" I replied sarcastically.

She could see perfectly well what I was doing. I was hunched over my little desk, writing a letter to my mother.

But Hope always has to poke her nose into everything.

She crossed the room and stood over my shoulder, reading my letter. I covered it up with one hand.

Hope laughed. A bitter laugh. "Eden, you're such a good girl," she said. "Writing home to Mom."

I didn't say anything. I knew that Hope didn't get along with her mother. She was always telling Angel,

Jasmine, and me such terrible stories about her childhood.

Behind me, Jasmine was sprawled on her bed, her face buried in a textbook, as usual. I didn't know where Angel was. Probably out with some guy. It was a safe bet.

Hope sighed. I started to write again, but she didn't go away. "Do you know what my mom used to call me?" she asked. "Do you know what my nickname was back home?"

"It couldn't be worse than Fish," Jasmine groaned.

I turned and caught the bitter expression on Hope's face. "She called me Buttertubs," she said through clenched teeth.

"Excuse me?" I cried, dropping my felt tip pen. "Why Buttertubs?"

Hope's eyes watered up, as if she were about to cry. "Because I was fat," she replied. "I wasn't even fat. I was a little chubby. Like I am now."

"And your mother called you Buttertubs?" I cried. "All the time?"

"Usually just when my friends were around," Hope said. She turned her face away and wiped the tears from her eyes. She didn't want me to see how much the memory upset her.

In some ways, Hope is very private.

Jasmine raised her head from her book. "She did that? Really? Your mom called you by that name in front of your friends?"

Hope nodded. "She loved embarrassing me. It was her only hobby."

She sighed again, crossed her arms in front of her blue sweater, and began pacing our small room. I followed her with my eyes.

Hope didn't look well. She hadn't brushed her hair. Her face, which normally had a rosy color, was kind of yellowy. And her eyes looked wet and sickly.

She was really upset and worried about Darryl, I knew. I could always tell. Whenever Hope got worked up about Darryl, she started talking about her mother.

Somehow the two were linked in her mind. Two bad news characters, I guess.

Except I knew that Hope really cared about Darryl.

"I don't know what made me think of Mom's nickname for me," Hope said, pacing the room. "But that wasn't the worst thing she did."

I realized Hope wasn't talking to Jasmine and me. She was actually talking to herself.

Jasmine lowered her head to her book. But I turned away from the desk to listen to Hope.

"Mom was so obsessed by my weight," Hope said, shaking her head. "She was as skinny as a rail. Really. She was as skinny as Angel. And I don't know why it bothered her so much that she had a chubby daughter. Maybe I looked like my dad or something. I don't know."

Jasmine raised her head again. "You don't know what your dad looked like?"

Hope shook her head. "I never met him. And Mom never kept any snapshots around." She let out a bitter laugh and started pacing again.

"One day I brought three kids home after school," Hope continued. "I guess I was in fourth or fifth grade. I don't remember."

She thought for a moment, then went on. "It was a hot day, and we were all hungry. So I took out a half-gallon box of ice cream from the freezer. And I dished out big bowls of chocolate ice cream for everyone.

"Well, we were all sitting around the kitchen table. We had just started eating the ice cream when Mom popped in. She looked around the table at my friends. Then she had a total fit that I was eating ice cream.

"She started screaming and carrying on, calling me Buttertubs in front of my friends. Then she grabbed up their ice cream bowls. Took the ice cream away from my friends and shoved all the bowls in front of me.

"'You like ice cream so much?' Mom screamed. 'Well, go ahead—eat them all.'

"She stood over me and forced me to eat all four bowls of ice cream," Hope continued, her mouth twisted angrily as she remembered the story.

"My friends wanted to leave. I mean, my mother was scaring them! But she made them all stay at the kitchen table and watch me.

"I started to cry. But Mom didn't care. She made me eat while I was crying. She made me eat all four bowls of ice cream while my friends stared in shock.

"Then, when I had choked down the last spoonful, Mom grabbed my head—and shoved my face into the ice cream carton. She pressed my head down and made me finish the carton. Made me lap it up—like a dog—until I'd finished it all."

I gasped. "You're kidding!"

But I could see by her expression that she wasn't kidding. The horrible story was true.

"Wow," Jasmine muttered from her bed. "Wow."

Hope turned her back to us. Her shoulders were trembling. She swept both hands back through her unbrushed blond hair.

"That's why I don't write home to Mom," she said in a choked whisper.

I gazed down at the letter I'd started.

Dear Mom, it said. *There's been a little trouble here at school. A boy was murdered outside our dorm. But I don't want you to worry. I think*

That's as far as I'd gotten.

"Hey—let's go out," Hope suggested. She forced a smile to her face. "Come on, guys. Some fresh air. Let's go."

"I can't," Jasmine said. "I have to finish this chapter. Besides, it's late."

Hope's face fell in disappointment. She turned to me. "How about you, Eden?"

I hesitated. I wanted to finish my letter and take a long, hot bath. But I decided that cheering up Hope was more important.

"Okay," I told her, jumping up. "I'll get a sweat-shirt. Let's go out."

That brought a smile to her face.

I crossed the room to my dresser and pulled out a blue-and-gold Ivy State sweatshirt. "Hope—what do you want to do?" I asked.

Her eyes flashed. "Get into trouble," she replied.

chapter

11

We walked a couple of blocks to the Blue Tavern. It's not really a tavern. It's more like a pizza joint that serves beer. It's one of the few places in town that stays open later than ten o'clock.

Just about every table was filled with kids from the college. The room smelled of cigarette smoke, pizza sauce, and beer. Blue ceiling lights cast a dark glow over everyone.

The restaurant has only blue lights. It's always dark and kind of gloomy inside. No matter what time of day you visit the Blue Tavern, it always seems like midnight.

Which, I guess, is why we like it.

Hope and I stood at the bar for a while, waiting for

a table to open up. We gazed around, peering through the smoky blue light, and didn't say much.

The waitresses, all dressed in short blue skirts and white blouses, scurried around. They carried pizzas and pitchers of beer on big metal trays, and struggled to squeeze through the crowded tables.

After about twenty minutes or so, a table against the back wall opened up. Hope and I grabbed it. We ordered a pizza as soon as the waitress came around.

"Hey—how's it going?"

Two guys at the next table grinned at us. I recognized one of them from my sociology class. He was kind of cute. He had very short, auburn hair and a little beard on his chin. And he had a nice smile.

His friend looked a little like a pirate. He had a red bandanna tied around his forehead, under a pile of curly, black hair.

"Hi," I called back.

Hope lowered her eyes to the table.

"What's up?" the cute one asked me.

I shrugged. "Just the usual."

I turned back to Hope. She had hunched down low, a fretful expression on her face. She kept her eyes down.

"What's your problem?" I asked. "Your posture gets worse every day."

She didn't smile at my joke. I suddenly realized that she *never* laughed or smiled at my jokes.

I crack jokes all the time. I mean, all the time. It's just the way I am. I think of myself as sort of sarcastic, sort of funny.

You *need* a sense of humor—right? It's my way of dealing with things. And people.

But until that moment, I'd never realized that I could *never* get even a smile from Hope.

What does she think of me? I suddenly wondered. Does she wish I'd stop making dumb jokes all the time?

"Hey—what's your name?" the bandanna guy called. He had to shout over the booming jukebox.

"Eden," I called back. "What's yours?"

"Gideon," came the reply.

He didn't look like a Gideon. I suddenly wondered what a good nickname for Gideon would be. Gid? Giddy?

Hope frowned and shook her head. "We'd better go," she murmured.

"Huh? Did you say go?" I leaned over the little table to hear her better.

A few tables away, some guy spilled a glass of beer. The glass shattered loudly on the floor. The guys all around burst out in applause and wild laughter.

So many grinning blue faces. That eerie blue glow washing over everyone.

"What's wrong, Hope?" I asked. "We just sat down. Our pizza isn't ready yet. Why do you want to leave?"

She raised her eyes to the front of the restaurant, but didn't reply.

I felt a sudden chill.

"Darryl?" I asked.

She nodded.

"Darryl is watching?" I asked. I turned and

squinted through the smoky blue haze. I didn't see him.

"He's watching," Hope said softly. I saw her chin quiver. "I don't want trouble, Eden."

"Hi." I heard a voice. Close by. And felt a hand on my shoulder.

I spun around to see the cute guy with the little beard grinning down at me. "You're in my sociology class," he said. "I'm Dave. He's Gideon." Gideon was also on his feet. Also grinning.

"Can we join you?" Dave asked.

"Well . . ." I hesitated. "I'm sorry, but my friend—"

Dave's smile faded. "What friend?" he asked.

"Huh?" I turned back to the table.

Hope had disappeared.

chapter

12

With a startled gasp, I jumped to my feet, nearly knocking the table over.

My eyes swept the restaurant. Squinting through the blue glare, I quickly searched for Hope.

Had Darryl appeared and dragged her off?

No. No way.

I would have heard him. I would have seen him.

Besides, Darryl would have no reason to be jealous. Unless . . .

Unless he saw us and thought we were here with Dave and Gideon.

Whoa. Slow down, I warned myself.

Hope saw Darryl across the tavern, and she ran over to say hi to him. That's all. That's all there is to it.

She isn't in trouble. She isn't in any danger.

Then why didn't she tell me she was leaving?

My heart pounded. I suddenly had a bad feeling about this.

I realized that the two guys were staring at me. "Are you okay?" Dave asked.

"Yeah. Fine," I replied. "My friend left, and I didn't realize . . ." My voice trailed off.

"Half plain, half pepperoni," a voice announced.

A blue-skirted waitress lowered a steaming-hot pizza to my table.

"I—I've got to go," I stammered.

The waitress didn't hear me. She was already on her way back to the kitchen.

"Aren't you going to eat?" Gideon asked. He eyed the pizza hungrily.

"Well . . ."

Hope is fine, I told myself.

I really liked Dave's smile.

I needed a guy in my life. A nice guy. Not a guy like Darryl. A guy with a little red beard and a nice smile. And a friend who looks like a dark-haired pirate.

I motioned for them to sit down. "My treat," I said, smiling at Dave. "If you'll buy a pitcher of Diet Coke."

"Oooh, Diet Coke! You sure you can handle it?" Dave teased. He and Gideon clicked glasses.

The three of us dove into the pizza. I was suddenly a lot hungrier than I thought.

We talked and laughed and had a good time.

I shoved Hope to the back of my mind. I kept

telling myself that she was probably back in the room safe and sound by now. Or off somewhere making out with Darryl.

Hope can take care of herself, I decided.

I tugged on Dave's beard. I just couldn't resist. "I had to see if it's a fake," I told him.

"The beard is real," he said. "The rest of my head is a fake!"

We laughed like lunatics at that. It wasn't that funny. But it was the way he said it.

I tugged his beard again, and we laughed some more.

Gideon said that his bandanna was holding his head together. We laughed at that too.

And finished off a second pizza.

The restaurant started to empty out. It was actually quiet enough now to talk without shouting. The blue light appeared to deepen. Dark purple shadows stretched over our table.

"Do you live on campus?" Dave asked me, finishing off our second pitcher of Diet Coke.

"Yeah. If you can call it living!" I joked. I swallowed a pepperoni, then shoved my plate away. I felt stuffed. And suddenly sleepy.

"I live in Fear Hall," I told them.

Both boys uttered exaggerated gasps. "Whoa! That's awesome!" Gideon cried.

"Have you ever seen any ghosts floating around in there?" Dave asked.

I squinted hard at him, trying to decide if he was serious or not. "Do you believe in ghosts?" I asked.

He shrugged. "I believe the stories about that dorm," he said seriously.

"Were you there the other night when that guy was murdered?" Gideon asked.

The question sent a chill down the back of my neck.

Hope. Hope and Darryl.

I was having such a good time, I'd forgotten all about my roommate.

I jumped up. "I've got to get back," I said. "I—I forgot something."

It took a few more minutes to say good-bye. Dave offered to study with me some evening soon. That made me happy. I really liked him. I was glad he wanted to see me again.

Both guys lived in an apartment west of campus. But they offered to walk me home.

I said no thanks. Fear Hall was only two blocks away. Besides, I felt like jogging back.

I was in a hurry now. I really wanted to make sure Hope was okay.

The cold night air shocked me. My skin felt hot and wet.

I knew I reeked of cigarette smoke. I had been so interested in Dave and Gideon, I hadn't realized how stuffy the restaurant was.

Leaning into the wind, I crossed the street and then started to jog. The cold air felt so refreshing against my face.

A car horn honked beside me, but I didn't turn. I kept jogging straight ahead, along the closed campus shops and restaurants.

I saw a couple leaning against a dark doorway, their arms around each other, kissing, not moving, still as statues. At first I thought it might be Hope and Darryl.

But as I trotted by, I didn't recognize them.

I wondered if Dave and I would ever kiss like that.

Back in the restaurant, when I tugged his beard, I'd had a strong impulse to pull his face to mine and give him a passionate kiss. Thinking about it made me smile.

A few seconds later, the high, dark brick walls of Fear Hall came into view. Gazing up, I saw that most of the rooms were dark. I had stayed at the Blue Tavern a lot longer than I'd realized.

I stepped into the building. Waved to Ollie, the old night guard, half asleep behind the front desk. And made my way to the elevators.

As the elevator rumbled up to thirteen, I crossed my fingers. *Please, Hope, be okay,* I thought.

I stepped out and gazed down the long hall. Two girls in pajamas were chatting at the far end. They leaned against the wall, talking quietly, both of them gesturing with their hands as they spoke.

One of the ceiling lights was out, leaving a pool of darkness in front of my room. Across the hall, I could hear music from the three M's room. Classical music.

I took a deep breath and turned the knob on my door. The door creaked open, and I peered inside.

A desk lamp against the far wall cast a triangle of yellow light on the floor. The other lights were all out.

I glimpsed Angel asleep in her lower bunk and heard Jasmine snore in the top bunk.

Then I saw Hope, huddled against her bed. Her eyes opened wide when she saw me. "Eden—" she whispered.

Before I could reply, Darryl stepped around the desk, into the triangle of light. He moved quickly, and I saw the scowl of anger on his face.

"I've been waiting for you, Eden," he growled.

"Darryl—what are you doing in here?" I demanded. "You know boys aren't allowed on this floor."

"Eden—don't get him angry," Hope warned in a trembling voice. She raised her hands and tugged at the sides of her blond hair.

I took a few steps toward him. I didn't feel afraid of him. I felt only anger.

What right did he have to barge into our room and try to frighten everyone?

Wasn't he grateful that we were protecting him? That we were keeping his horrible crime a secret?

"What's your problem, Darryl?" I asked through clenched teeth.

He picked up a sheet of paper from the desk. His face was in shadow, but his pale blue eyes glowed. "Did you write this?" he demanded.

I stared at it. "What is that? The letter I started?"

He nodded.

"Give it to me!" I screamed. "You have no right to read my letters. You have no right—"

I rushed forward and tried to swipe it from his hand.

But he reached out with his other hand and grabbed my wrist.

"Oww! Let go!" I tried to squirm free.

But he bent my arm behind my back. Jerked it hard. And kept bending it until I screamed again.

"What else were you going to write, Eden?" Darryl whispered in my ear. His hot breath swept over my face. Made my skin prickle.

"Nothing—" I choked out. "Let go. You're *hurting* me!"

"Let go of her!" Hope shouted.

"What else were you going to write in your letter?" Darryl repeated. "Were you going to tell your mom about me? Were you going to tell her who did that terrible thing in front of the dorm?"

He twisted my arm back until I shrieked in pain.

"No. No—of course not!" I whispered.

He let out an angry snarl—and shoved me hard against the wall.

I spun around, breathing hard. My shoulder throbbed with pain.

He balled up the letter and tossed it at me. It hit my forehead and bounced to the floor.

A grin spread over his face. A grin of triumph.

And that's when I decided to kill him.

chapter

13

W ell . . . no.

I didn't want to kill him. I just wanted to get rid of him.

I wanted to get him out of our lives. I wanted to call the police and tell them what he had done.

I wanted Darryl away. Far away, where I'd never have to be afraid of him again.

A hard knock on the door made us all jump.

Darryl dove for the bathroom. Hope followed. He slammed the door behind them.

Angel sleepily raised her head from her pillow. "Who's here?" she asked, blinking. Then she turned her face to the wall. Jasmine remained sound asleep in the top bunk.

I had left the door open a crack. As I took a step

59

toward it, it swung open. Melanie and Mary poked their heads in.

"Is everything okay?" Mary asked.

I picked up my balled-up letter from the floor. "Yeah. What's wrong?" I replied.

"We . . . heard voices," Melanie said. "We wondered . . ."

"I'm sorry. Did I have the radio on too loud?" I asked, thinking quickly.

Melanie's eyes lowered to the boom box on the windowsill. "But the radio isn't on," she said, eyeing me suspiciously.

"I—uh—turned it off when you knocked," I told her. "I'm really sorry if it was too loud. I—"

"Mary and I have just been so freaked," Melanie said, tugging at her single, dangling earring. "I mean—since Brendan was murdered."

"We jump at every sound," Mary added. "None of us can sleep. Margie thinks she flunked her French test yesterday. We're all totally freaked."

"We are too," I told her.

Both girls narrowed their eyes at me. Studying me. They exchanged glances.

Did I say something wrong? I wondered.

Why are they *looking* at me like that?

"It's so frightening," Melanie said finally. "We can't relax in our own dorm room."

"We were trying to study," Mary added. "But we thought we heard a boy's voice. From your room. So . . ." Her voice trailed off.

"A boy? Up here?" I cried. I shook my head. "I don't think so."

I glanced at the bathroom door. I had a strong urge to tell Melanie and Mary, "Look in the bathroom. You'll find a boy in there. You'll find a *murderer* in there!"

But I bit my bottom lip and remained silent.

"It must have been the radio," Melanie said quietly. "Sorry."

They started back to their room. But at the door, Mary turned back to me. "We're trying to organize a meeting," she told me.

"A meeting?"

"Some kind of safety meeting," Mary said. "You know. To talk about how we can protect ourselves. And maybe force the college to get more security for the dorm. Some more guards."

"Ollie is a sweet old guy. But he isn't much of a guard. He's usually asleep at his desk," Melanie complained. "Anyone can walk right by him."

I nodded. "That's true."

Mary chuckled. "Someone told me a story about Ollie. They said he died thirty years ago. But his ghost refused to leave Fear Hall. He takes his guard post every night, even though he's dead."

I forced a laugh. "It's probably true. He *looks* dead."

"It isn't funny," Melanie said sharply. "People think Fear Hall is a joke. A place for ghost stories. But the truth is, a boy we all knew died right outside the front door. And the college hasn't done anything at all to make sure the rest of us are safe."

"So you'll come to the meeting?" Mary asked.

"Sure," I told her, glancing again at the bathroom door. "We'll all come."

Once again, their expressions changed. They stared at me as if I'd said something wrong.

What is their *problem?* I wondered.

"You sure you're okay?" Melanie asked.

"Sure," I told her. I yawned. "Just a little sleepy. See you guys tomorrow."

They said good night and made their way across the hall to 13-A. I closed my door and leaned against it. I took a deep breath. "Strange," I muttered to myself. "Very strange."

The next day was even stranger.

chapter
_____
14

*T*he next morning, I ran into Dave on my way to history class. He flashed me that cute smile of his. It was a cold, blustery day. But his smile made me feel warm all over.

Despite the sharp winds that blew across The Triangle, he had his leather jacket open, revealing a red-and-green flannel shirt underneath.

He looked so warm and cuddly. I had a sudden impulse to wrap my arms around him.

"How's it going, Eden?" he asked. "You recovered from all those Diet Cokes last night?"

We both laughed.

"I'm late for history class," I told him, gazing up at the gray, stone Fine Arts building across The Triangle.

"How about a cup of coffee after your class?" he asked. The wind whipped his red hair.

"Okay. I'll meet you here," I replied. I shifted my backpack on my shoulders, turned, and hurried to class.

Mr. Cumberland, the professor, gazed up from his papers as I slid into my seat. He's a balding, middle-aged man who wears a gray sweater every day over baggy chinos.

He has tiny, frameless reading glasses perched on the end of his nose. He's always peering over the glasses to talk to us. It makes him look like a near-sighted owl.

I'm very interested in the course, Nineteenth-Century History. I think life was so interesting a hundred years ago.

Hope is always teasing me about it. She says, "Eden, you can't go back in time. If you lived a hundred years ago, you'd be dead already!"

Unfortunately, Mr. Cumberland is not a very interesting teacher. Most of the time, he stands behind his desk and reads from his lecture notes. He never lets us ask questions. In fact, he barely speaks to his students at all.

The only time he ever seems to notice us is when he goes over his seating chart. Yes. I know it's strange. But he has a seating chart for us—just like a teacher in an elementary school.

I pulled out my notebook and turned to a clean page. I couldn't find my pen, so I borrowed one from the girl next to me.

THE BEGINNING

When I turned to the front, Mr. Cumberland was moving along the rows of desks. He appeared to be checking off names on his seating chart.

He stopped in front of my desk and peered down at me over those tiny, frameless glasses. Then his eyes moved to the chart in his hand. "You're Hope Mathis?"

"No," I told him. "I'm Eden Leary."

He squinted down at his chart. "You're not Hope Mathis?"

I shook my head. "She's my roommate," I told him.

Everyone was staring at me. I suddenly felt uncomfortable.

Why was Hope's name on his chart?

She didn't take this course. I'd been here since the beginning of the semester.

So why would Hope's name show up on the seating chart?

"Eden Leary . . ." Mr. Cumberland murmured. Squinting through the little glasses, his eyes swept over the rows of boxes on the chart.

"Have you been sitting in for your roommate?" he asked.

"No," I replied. I could feel my face grow hot and knew I was blushing. "I don't know how her name got on your chart. She doesn't take this course."

"Let me check my enrollment list," Mr. Cumberland said, scratching his bald head. He turned and made his way to his desk, taking long strides.

Then he shuffled through a stack of papers. Pulled one out. And studied it.

"Eden Leary . . ." He repeated my name.

I heard kids whispering. A few were staring at me. Others were skimming through the history text.

"I'm sorry, Miss Leary," Mr. Cumberland said finally. He frowned at me.

"Sorry?" I repeated.

"You don't seem to be enrolled in my class," he announced.

"But that's impossible!" I cried. My voice broke. I could feel myself blush again. "I've been here all semester."

"That may be true," Mr. Cumberland replied quietly. "But you are not on the enrollment list. And you are not on the seating chart."

"But—but—" I sputtered. "What does that mean? It's just some kind of a mistake."

"Yes, I'm sure." He nodded. "Perhaps you could go straighten it out with the dean."

I realized my heart was pounding. "You mean—I have to leave?" I cried.

He nodded again. "Please get this matter straightened out. I'm sure it's all a computer mix-up. Whenever anything goes wrong these days, it's a computer mix-up."

I handed the pen back to the girl next to me. She flashed me a sympathetic smile.

I picked up my backpack and shoved the textbook into it. My hands were trembling. I felt really upset.

"You sure I'm not in this course?" I asked.

"I don't have your name," Mr. Cumberland replied. "I'm really sorry."

He turned away from me and picked up his lecture notes. "Today we will begin our study of the early labor movement," he announced.

I hoisted up my backpack and slunk out of the room. I saw kids watching me. A couple of them shook their heads, as if I had been caught cheating or something. As if I was some kind of criminal.

My head spun as I stepped out of the Fine Arts building, back into the cold. I blinked in the glare of bright sunlight.

I *am* in that course, I told myself. *Aren't* I?

Is it really possible that I shouldn't be there? Is it actually Hope's class?

Then why isn't Hope there? Why have I been there all year?

Have I really been going to the wrong class?

How could I be so confused?

The bright yellow light shimmered in waves over the grass of The Triangle. I suddenly felt dizzy. I shut my eyes, but the light still shimmered against my eyelids.

So much to think about, I told myself. So much to worry about.

It's Darryl's fault.

I'm so frightened of him. I spend so much time thinking about him, how evil he is.

I can't think straight at all.

I've got to do something about Darryl. I've *got* to.

I opened my eyes. A cloud rolled over the sun. A shadow swept over the classroom buildings that lined The Triangle. The gusting wind felt even colder.

I'm going to call the police now, I decided.

I'm going to find a phone and call them. And tell them about Darryl. Then I won't have to worry about him anymore.

Then I'll be able to think straight again.

I turned and made my way back into the Fine Arts building. I remembered seeing a row of pay phones in the front lobby.

My shoes clicked on the marble floor. My eyes adjusted slowly to the dimmer light. I spotted the phones at the back wall and trotted over to them.

What shall I say? I wondered. "I'm calling from Ivy State? I know who murdered that boy in front of Fear Hall?"

Yes.

Might as well get right to the point.

I stepped up to the first phone. I took a deep breath and lifted the receiver.

I raised my finger to push 0 for the operator.

But a hand grabbed my hand and tugged it away.

Darryl!

chapter

15

No. Not Darryl.

Hope.

"Oh—!" I let out a startled cry.

She let go of my hand. "Sorry. I didn't mean to scare you, Eden. I thought you saw me."

"No, I—" I let out a long sigh of relief. I was so glad to see Hope and not Darryl.

Her brown eyes studied me. "I thought you had a class right now."

"I—I did," I replied. "But there was some kind of weird mix-up."

I returned the phone receiver to its hook.

She pulled a brown leaf from her hair and crumpled it in her fingers. "A mix-up?"

"Are you enrolled in a history class this semester?" I asked her.

Hope shook her head. "No. You know my schedule, Eden. You're the history major in the group. Not me."

"So it *is* a mix-up," I declared. "The professor had your name instead of mine."

"Weird," she replied. "Why would he have my name? They must have made a mistake in the registration office."

Her eyes moved to the phone booth. "Who were you calling, Eden?"

I hesitated. "Uh . . . well . . ."

She waited.

"Can I tell you the truth, Hope?" I asked. I didn't wait for an answer. "I was calling the police. I can't keep the secret about Darryl any longer. I'm sorry. I just can't."

The words poured out of me like a waterfall. I knew Hope wouldn't be happy about my decision. But I didn't care. I had made up my mind.

The light in her eyes faded, as if a cloud had washed over them. Her chin quivered. "You mean you weren't going to ask me first?"

I stared back at her. "No."

"You weren't going to tell me? You weren't going to give me any warning?" Her voice grew shrill and angry. "You were just going to make the call?"

"I . . . have to do it, Hope," I stammered. "I can't keep the secret. It's making me too crazy. I—I'm frightened all the time."

"But you know how important Darryl is to me!" Hope cried. She grabbed the sleeves of my jacket and held on as if grasping a life preserver. "Please, Eden . . ."

"I don't know what to say," I confessed. "I know you love Darryl. I know what he means to you. But he's no good, Hope. He did a horrible thing. He . . . he killed another human being. He deserves to pay."

"How about waiting just a little bit longer?" Hope pleaded, still holding my jacket sleeves. "How about we talk about it tonight? All four of us. We talk about it, and we vote. Is that okay, Eden?"

She didn't give me a chance to reply. "We'll have a fair vote," she continued frantically. "I'll go along with whatever is decided. I promise. I just don't think it's right for you to decide on your own. I mean, we're all in this together—right?"

I swallowed hard. I still didn't reply.

"Right, Eden?" Hope insisted. "Right? Right?"

Glancing through the glass door, I saw Dave waiting for me out on The Triangle. He had his hands shoved in his jacket pockets. He paced back and forth along the narrow walk that cut through the grass.

"Okay," I told Hope. "I'll wait."

"Thank you!" she cried. She wrapped me in a tight hug.

"I've got to go," I said. "Talk to you later."

"Yes. Later," she replied.

I hurried to the door. Dave was still pacing in front of the building.

I waved to him. Pushed open the doors. Called to him as I rushed outside. "Dave—hi!"

If only I hadn't listened to Hope. If only I had stayed and made that call . . .

If only I had turned Darryl in to the police . . .

I might have saved Dave's life.

chapter

16

That evening, Dave and I went out to dinner. The plan was to grab a quick, early bite and then go to the library to study.

We walked to Murphy's, a coffee shop a few blocks from the campus. The cold winds had vanished, and the air felt warm and sweet. Almost springlike.

Back in Fear Hall, I'd had a terrible time deciding what to wear. It was kind of like a first date, and I wanted to look just right.

I didn't want to dress up at all. I mean, I had to look casual. I had to look like myself. But I didn't want to look as if I didn't care how I looked.

The usual panic time.

Until Hope offered to lend me her black silk top

and short black skirt. I found a pair of dark purple tights—and I was set.

I checked myself out in the closet door mirror. "Awesome," I told myself. Sexy, but not trying too hard.

I met Dave downstairs. He was talking with two girls I'd seen around the dorm. They all laughed about something. Then one of them gave Dave a playful shove.

Watching them, I felt instantly jealous. Both girls seemed to know Dave better than I did.

I also felt a little disappointed that he hadn't dressed up at all. He was wearing the same jeans and oversized flannel shirt he wore in sociology class that afternoon.

But when he smiled at me, I forgot all of my complaints.

I really like this guy, I realized as I hurried across the dorm lobby to him. I really want this to work out.

"Hey—you look great," he said, his smile growing wider.

"My roommate lent me this," I admitted, gesturing to the top and skirt.

He laughed. "That's the best kind of roommate. A roommate who's the same size as you are!"

He pulled a piece of lint from my hair. His fingers brushed my forehead. My skin tingled where he had touched me.

We stepped out into the warm evening and made our way toward the coffee shop. Some kids were flying kites on The Triangle. Two red dragon kites had become tangled. They appeared to wrestle each other, their heads bobbing and ducking in their silent fight.

A blue Frisbee came flying toward us. Dave jumped high and brought it down. He flipped it back to its owner, who came running across the grass.

"It's really like spring," Dave said, grinning. "It's awesome. Everyone has spring fever—and it's nearly winter!"

"I love it," I said, taking his arm.

As we approached the front of Murphy's, the three M's—Melanie, Mary, and Margie—came walking out. "Hey, Hope—how's it going?" Melanie called.

I laughed. "It's me! I'm only wearing her clothes!" I called back.

Mary said something to Margie I couldn't hear. They waved and hurried off.

Dave held open the restaurant door for me.

"This is my day for being mistaken for Hope," I grumbled. "I really don't think we look that much alike—do we?"

Dave shrugged and followed me inside. "I've never met Hope," he replied. "But I'm sure you're much better looking."

I laughed. And slid into a booth against the wall. "Flattery will get you everywhere," I teased.

We had a nice dinner. I felt so comfortable and relaxed with Dave. We talked and laughed together, as if we'd known each other for a long time.

I told him about Hope, and Angel, and Jasmine. How different we all are. But how close we've become.

And I told him about the mix-up in history class this morning. How embarrassed I was that I had to leave.

"Did you get it straightened out?" Dave asked.

"I didn't have a chance," I told him. "I'm going to go see the dean tomorrow morning."

Dave talked about Michael, his older brother. He said he was worried about Michael.

Michael had been a champion basketball player in college. He had articles written about him in *Sports Illustrated,* and he was always talked about on TV sports shows.

He was a great college player—but he wasn't tall enough or strong enough to play in the NBA. Michael graduated last spring, Dave told me. And he hasn't done anything since.

He misses being a star. He misses all the attention, all the cheers and applause.

"It's like his life is already over," Dave said sadly. "He was a superstar in college. Now there's nowhere for him to go but down."

Dave's expression changed. "That's why I'm glad I'm such a big nothing. I have no talents and no skills. So I'm a happy guy."

He laughed.

"Hey, that's not true!" I protested.

"Oh, really?" he teased. "What talent do I have?"

"Well . . ." I grinned at him. "You can grow a very cute beard."

76

I tugged at the red fuzz under his chin.

He pretended to be insulted. "Cute? Cute? Do you really think I was trying for *cute?*" He slapped my hand away. "Stop pulling on it. It isn't glued on that well."

It felt so great to be sitting in this restaurant, laughing and joking with such a sweet guy. I wondered if he really liked me. I wondered if we'd start to see a lot of each other.

I knew I wasn't as pretty as Jasmine. And I wasn't as slinky and sexy as Angel.

But Dave didn't seem to mind.

After we had our second cup of coffee, we split the check. Then we made our way outside.

The sun had set while we were in the restaurant. The sky was a deep purple with traces of pink. The air still felt warm and springlike.

The streetlights hadn't come on. Lights from store windows spilled over the sidewalk. Car headlights swept brightly over the building fronts.

"It's too nice out to go study in a stuffy library," Dave said, gazing up at the sky.

I walked close beside him. "What do you want to do?"

Before he could answer, a figure leaped out from the side of a shoe store.

His face was hidden in shadow. His body was covered by a long raincoat, down nearly to the ground.

"Hey—" I cried out as he hurtled into Dave.

Diving from the darkness, the figure lowered his shoulder—and smashed it hard into Dave's stomach.

Dave uttered a startled groan. Grabbed his stomach.

And staggered limply back against the wall.

"Nooooo!" he pleaded—as the figure prepared to attack again.

chapter
_____
17

I froze in horror.

Dave raised his hands above his head to protect himself.

A car roared around the corner. Its headlights rolled over the tall figure in the raincoat.

He tossed back his head, grinning, eyes flashing.

"Gideon!" Dave cried angrily. "You creep!"

"Huh?" I gasped, squinting into the darkness. Yes. It was Dave's friend from the restaurant. Not wearing a bandanna. But I recognized him now.

Dave lurched away from the building and wrapped his hands around Gideon's throat. "You creep!" he repeated. "You scared me to death!" He pretended to strangle his friend.

Gideon laughed and pulled away. The long raincoat

swirled around him. "You were so scared, your beard flew off!"

"Where did you come from?" Dave demanded.

"Cleveland," Gideon joked. He laughed at his own joke. "No. Actually, I was walking by. On my way to a friend's apartment. I saw you two in Murphy's. So I decided to wait for you. Give you a little surprise."

He turned and seemed to notice me for the first time. "Hi, Eden." He pushed back his black hair, then straightened the collar on the big raincoat.

"You scared me too," I confessed.

"I'm a scary guy," Gideon replied.

"Want to come with us?" Dave suggested. "Eden and I were trying to think of a way to avoid going to the library."

Gideon snickered. "I can think of a *lot* of ways for a guy and a girl to avoid the library."

"Maybe we'll go to that driving range on Fulton," Dave said, ignoring Gideon's meaning. "Hit a few buckets." He turned to me. "Do you play golf?"

"Well, no," I replied. "But I've always wanted to try it."

"I'm a great teacher," Dave said. He put his hands together in a golf grip, leaned forward, and swung an invisible club. Then he turned to Gideon. "How about it? You coming?"

Gideon shook his head. "I should. I could give you a few pointers. But I told you, I'm on my way to my friend's apartment. You remember Joanne. From back home."

He glanced at his watch. "I'm only half an hour late."

Dave rolled his eyes. "That's right on time for you."

"Later," Gideon called, hurrying off, his raincoat flapping behind him.

"I owe him one," Dave murmured, watching his friend vanish around the corner. "I owe him a good scare. My heart is still pounding."

Dave and I were the only ones at the driving range. The young man in the tiny clubhouse gave us a bucket of golf balls. But he told us to hit them quickly. He wanted to close up.

I started to pick up a club from the rack against the wall. But Dave stopped me.

"Not that one," he instructed. "That's a wood. You're not ready for a wood yet."

"A wood? But it's made out of metal!" I protested.

"It's still called a wood," Dave replied. He handed me a smaller club. "This is a five iron. Let's start with this."

Carrying the bucket of golf balls, he led the way along the row of empty booths. Bright spotlights made the field glow brighter than daylight. A heavy dew had fallen. The grass shone wetly at our feet.

"We'll start out by learning the grip," Dave announced, stopping at the very last tee. "Then I'll show you how to swing."

He dropped a handful of balls to the grass. "Watch me a few times."

He took the club, gripped it, placing his hands carefully, holding them up so I could see. Then he leaned over the ball. Took a few short practice swings. Pulled his shoulders back—and hit the ball.

I squinted into the bright light and watched it sail up and off to the right.

Dave grinned at me. "Not very good. I'm a little rusty."

He motioned for me to step over to the tee. I picked up the club he had given me and started over to him.

But something made me stop.

A sound.

A feeling. A feeling that we were no longer alone.

I spun around—and saw him, saw his pale eyes, his features tight with anger.

"Darryl!" I choked out. "Darryl—what are you *doing* here?"

chapter

18

"The most important thing to remember," Dave was saying, "is not to move your head."

Dave had his back to me. He didn't see Darryl move toward us.

"Darryl—please!" I cried. "It's me—Eden. I'm just wearing Hope's outfit!"

Darryl ignored me. His eyes lowered to the club in my hand.

I raised it, as if to fight him off.

But he snatched it away with one hand. Grabbed it and pushed me aside.

"Dave—!" I tried to warn him.

But he had his head lowered, his body arched, preparing to swing again.

"Dave—!" I screamed.

83

Too late.

Darryl raised the metal club—pulled it back and swung it like a baseball bat.

Swung it at Dave's head.

The club made a solid *thunnnk* as it hit. And then I heard a disgusting ripping sound.

"Ohhhhh!" I uttered a horrified moan as the club caught Dave behind the ear.

The ripping sound . . . the horrible ripping . . . like Velcro being pulled apart . . .

And Dave's ear sailed up . . . up . . . into the bright glare of the spotlights.

I turned my eyes away before it came down.

Dave let out a roar. A roar of pain. Of shock.

Blood gushed out the side of his head. Eyes bulging, mouth open, Dave raised his hand to cover the hole.

But Darryl swung again.

This time the club caught Dave's cheek.

Dave cried out again. Dropped to his knees.

"Nooooooo!" An animal wail burst from my throat. "Darryl—noooooo!"

Darryl swung again. The club grazed the top of Dave's head, scraping off a patch of his auburn hair.

"Please! Pleeeeeease!" I moaned.

Dave was hunched on his knees. Rocking back and forth. Hands raised. Blood dripping from his head. Flowing down his jacket.

Darryl pulled the club back. He let out a groan as he swung once again with all his strength.

The club smashed into Dave's throat.

He uttered a choked gurgle.

THE BEGINNING

His eyes rolled up in his head. And he crumbled facedown in the blood-stained grass.

"Darryl—no! No! *No!*"

I watched helplessly as Darryl swung again. Again. Beating Dave's unmoving body.

"No! No! No!"

I spun away. I couldn't watch anymore.

My stomach lurched. I started to sway over.

Caught my balance.

And struggled to run.

Away. Got to get away.

My shoes slipping over the silvery, wet grass.

I ran. Covered in blood. Covered in Dave's warm blood.

I ran

And didn't look back.

part four

Hope

chapter

19

I hugged Eden. I let her cry on my shoulder. I held her for the longest time.

"Hope . . . Hope . . ." she repeated my name like some kind of sad chant.

I took her into the bathroom. I helped her get out of her blood-soaked clothes. *My* blood-soaked clothes.

I helped her wash the caked blood from her hair.

She trembled so hard, she couldn't do anything for herself. She was helpless. Completely helpless.

"We have to stop him," Eden whispered as I helped her into her nightshirt. "He killed Dave. We have to stop him."

"I want to tell you a story," I said, trying to sound calm. I kept my voice low and steady.

I guided her to her bed. I kept my arm around her trembling shoulders. I tried to soothe her.

"I don't want to hear a story, Hope," Eden choked out. "I want to call the police—*now.*"

I tucked her into bed. "It's a short story," I said softly. "Lie back, Eden. Close your eyes. You've had a terrible shock."

"Darryl is crazy," she whispered. A single tear ran down her cheek. "Crazy. Did he really think I was you? Is that why he killed Dave? Is it?"

"Eden—sshhhh," I replied. I smoothed my hand over her light-brown hair. "Take a deep breath. You're okay. You're safe and sound now."

"But Dave—" A sob escaped her throat. She jerked herself up from the pillow. "Call the police now, Hope. Please—do it now."

"I can't," I said, keeping my voice low and soothing. "Let me tell you my story, Eden. It's a very short story."

She settled back on the pillow. Her chest heaved up and down. She whimpered quietly with each breath.

Smoothing my hand through her hair, I started my story. "When I was a kid, my mother used to buy all my clothes for me. Even in high school, she wouldn't allow me to choose what I wore.

"I know that sounds kind of mean. Because all kids like to have a say about what they wear. But, believe me, Eden, choosing all my clothes wasn't the meanest thing my mother did.

"The meanest thing was the size she picked out for

me. You see, my mother always bought my clothes a size too small. I'm not talking about one or two items. I mean *everything* I ever wore.

"All of my skirts, all of my tops and T-shirts, all of my jeans. Even my shoes. Year after year—my whole childhood—I had to squeeze into my clothes.

"When I was a six, my mother bought me all fours. And when I was a ten, she bought me eights. And if I protested, if I made a fuss about the size, she threatened to take the clothes away and leave me nothing at all to wear.

"And so I got used to squeezing into my clothes, Eden," I continued, trying not to reveal my anger, trying to keep my voice calm. "I got used to always being uncomfortable. Always looking gross and ridiculous.

"I got used to being unhappy," I said. "And do you know why my mother did it? Do you know why she always made me wear clothes that were too small for me? You know the answer, don't you?

"Because she thought I was too fat. And she never wanted me to forget it for a minute. Every time I got dressed, I was reminded. Every time . . ."

My voice trailed off. I couldn't go on. So many bad memories. So many horrible things I held inside.

"Why . . . ?" Eden murmured, staring up at me. "Hope—why did you tell me that story tonight?"

"Haven't you guessed?" I asked softly. "I told you that story because Darryl is the first person in my life who doesn't care that I am overweight."

"But, Hope—" Eden started.

I smoothed her hair. Gently. Keeping a steady rhythm.

"He's the only one who ever liked me just the way I am," I told her. "And that means so much to me. It means *everything* to me. I can't give him up that easily. Do you understand, Eden?

"I can't give him up no matter what he does," I confessed. "Because he's the only one I've got."

Eden whispered a reply. I couldn't hear her. I wiped a tear from my eye. I hadn't even realized I'd been crying.

I sat beside Eden's bed, soothing her, trying to comfort her. I'm not sure how long.

Finally, she fell into a fitful sleep.

I gazed down at her, watching the rise and fall of her chest beneath the covers, listening to her shallow breathing.

And then a voice from behind me rasped, "Okay, Hope. Go ahead. You can strangle her now."

chapter
20

I whirled around. "Darryl—" I whispered.

He stood behind me, breathing hard, his hair wild, his sweatshirt stained with dark blood.

"Get out!" I cried. "I mean it. Get out! Get down to your room."

"She saw me, Hope," Darryl whispered, gazing down at Eden, his eyes red-rimmed. Crazy eyes. "She saw me. I can't let her live. I can't trust her. I have to—"

He reached out both hands as if to strangle her.

I shoved him away.

"Get out," I repeated. "Get out now, Darryl. Leave Eden alone. And go away."

"I want to tell you what happened," he insisted. "I saw your clothes. I saw that other boy. I—"

"Just leave," I said firmly, staring him down.

"I have to explain," he protested. "Hope—you've always listened to me before. Give me a chance."

He pulled me to my feet. He slid his arms around my waist and held me close. "You've always listened to me," he whispered. "You've always understood."

I let him hold me for a moment. Then I lifted his hands and pushed him away. "Darryl, there's nothing to explain," I whispered.

His mouth dropped open. He swept his thick, auburn hair off his forehead. "No. I want to explain. Give me a chance, Hope."

I glanced down at Eden, sleeping so lightly. Whimpering in her sleep.

"Explain," I told Darryl. "Go ahead."

He stared back at me, his mouth still open. Blood had caked on his neck. On his chin.

"Explain," I repeated, challenging him.

His expression changed. He stood tensely. He swept his hair back again. "I—I can't explain." He sighed. "You're right. There is no explanation. I lost it, Hope. That's all."

His eyes locked on mine. "What can I do?" he asked. He sounded like a lost little boy. "What can I do now, Hope? Tell me."

"Go downstairs to your room," I instructed him.

He nodded obediently.

"You don't want to be caught up here on the girls'

floor," I continued. "Especially with that blood caked all over you."

He rubbed the front of his sweatshirt.

"Get rid of all your clothes," I told him. "Put them all in a bag. Toss it in the incinerator. Then get yourself cleaned up. Take a long, hot bath."

He nodded again. "Then what?"

I shrugged. "I don't know."

He lowered his gaze to Eden. "What do we do about her? We can't let her tell the police."

"I'll deal with Eden," I promised.

"How?" Darryl cried. "How? If she turns me in, Hope, they'll take me away forever. We'll never see each other again."

"We—we can't talk about that now," I stammered. I felt a sharp stab of anger. "You should have thought of that before," I told Darryl. "Before you started killing people."

The light in his eyes faded. "I only did it for you," he murmured, turning away.

And then he turned back to me, his mouth curled in a defiant sneer. "And I'll kill again, Hope. I promise I will. Tell that to your friend Eden. I won't let anyone separate you and me. Tell her I'll kill again if I have to."

His words sent a tremor of fear down my body.

I couldn't let him kill again.

But what could I do? How could I stop him?

chapter

21

The clock radio woke me up at eight the next morning. And the first thing I heard was a news report about Eden's friend.

I sat up, feeling cold all over. A deep chill.

Instantly wide awake, the words rang through my mind. And stayed there. I remember every word the radio reporter said:

"The slashed and mutilated body of an Ivy State student was found late last night at the Garrison Corners Driving Range near the campus. The student's name is being withheld until police can notify his parents.

"Police are seeking a young woman for questioning. The attendant on duty at the driving range saw the young woman with the murder victim.

"Since this is the second vicious murder of a student in the past two weeks, police have opened a widespread investigation. College officials are meeting this morning to discuss how to deal with frightened students."

The words sent chill after chill down my back. I sat up stiffly in bed. Picturing Darryl. Picturing the poor dead boy.

Eden's friend.

The police were looking for Eden.

I tried to shake off my chills.

Eden . . . Eden . . . Eden . . .

I turned toward her bed. She lay on her side, snoring lightly. One arm trailed down over the bed, her light-brown hair tumbling over her face.

I knew what Eden would do as soon as she woke up. As soon as she heard the police were looking for her.

She would go to them. She would go to the police station and tell them everything. She would turn in Darryl. And describe what Darryl had done.

And I would never see Darryl again. Never see the only boy who ever cared about me.

"I can't let you do that, Eden," I murmured aloud.

I climbed up from bed. Stretched. Straightened my nightshirt.

Then I crossed to Eden's bed and shook her shoulders gently. "Eden—wake up. We have to talk."

She awoke with a start. Blinked her eyes wide. "Huh?" She stared up at me as if she didn't recognize me. As if she didn't know where she was.

"It's me," I said. "I have to talk to you."

"Oh." She cleared her throat. "Oh, wow. Hope—I was having the *worst* dream."

I sighed. "Real life is probably scarier than your dream," I said sadly.

She sat up slowly. I could practically see the thoughts running through her mind. I could see her remembering . . . reliving the horrifying scene at the driving range.

The radio news droned on in the background. The distant, high wail of a siren floated in from the open window.

"Dave . . ." Eden said softly. Her voice was still hoarse from sleep. She cleared her throat again and turned to me. "Hand me the phone, Hope."

I didn't move. "Why?" I demanded.

"I have to call the police," she replied firmly.

"We have to talk about this," I insisted. I put a hand on her shoulder. But she brushed it away.

"There's nothing to talk about," she replied sadly. Her eyes were dull. Dead. She spoke lifelessly, almost as if talking in her sleep.

"I can't think straight," she continued. "I can't think at all. I can't think of anything but Dave. And Darryl. Darryl being so vicious. Like a wild, ferocious animal."

She took a deep breath. "Hand me the phone, Hope."

I shook my head. "No. Wait, Eden."

"Wait? Wait for what?" she demanded sharply. She lowered her feet to the floor. Her hands gripped the bedspread tightly, tensely.

"I don't want you to turn Darryl in," I said, slowly, softly. "Not yet, anyway."

"I don't have a choice," Eden said in a trembling voice. "I really don't."

"Let *me* deal with Darryl," I urged. "Let me get him the help he needs."

"Help? *Help?*" A scornful laugh burst from Eden's throat. "He doesn't need *help.* He needs to be locked up. He needs to be put away—forever."

"Eden, please, listen—" I pleaded.

But she jumped up. Pushed me aside. Moved toward the desk, her bare feet thudding on the carpet.

"He's a dangerous animal, Hope," she said, her jaw clenched. "He's a *vicious* animal."

I hurried up beside her. She reached for the phone on the desk. But I pulled her hand away.

"Wait. Let me tell you a story," I pleaded. "It won't take long. Then—"

She let out a shriek. "No! No more stories, Hope! It's too late for stories."

She turned to me and put her hands on my shoulders. She brought her face close to mine. Her eyes burned into me. "I know how you feel," she uttered in a trembling voice. "At least I think I do."

"No, you don't," I insisted. "If you did—"

"I know how much you care about Darryl," she continued. "I know how much you want to be with him."

Her expression hardened. "But it's time for a reality check, Hope. It's time for you to realize that you *can't* protect Darryl. You can't protect him, and you can't hide him. He has to pay for what he's done. And you'll just have to get over him."

"No . . . No, Eden. *Please*—" I begged.

But she picked up the phone and raised it to her ear. She pressed 0.

I can't let her! I told myself.

My heart thudded in my chest. The room started to tilt and sway.

I can't let her make this call!

"Eden—please!" I felt so dizzy. The room bounced and tilted, as if we were in an earthquake. As if my whole world was falling apart . . .

"Eden—!"

She ignored me. Turned her back. Pressed the phone to her ear. "Hello? Operator?"

Frantic, I whirled around.

Picked up Angel's hair dryer.

Grabbed it by the nozzle—and swung the heavy handle at Eden's head.

It connected with a loud *thonnnnk.*

Her skull made a cracking sound. Like eggshells breaking.

Eden groaned.

Her eyes shot open in shock. Then they rolled up into her head.

With another groan, she slumped lifelessly to the carpet.

She sprawled on her stomach, one leg bent beneath her.

The phone fell from her hand and bounced across the floor.

"Ohhh." I dropped the heavy hair dryer. Pressed my hands against the sides of my face.

And stared down at my friend's unmoving body. Stared in disbelief.

"What have I done?" I shrieked.

"What have I done?"

chapter

22

*E*den groaned.

Her hands twitched.

"Oh, thank goodness!" I cried.

I hadn't killed her. She was alive. She'd only been stunned.

I knelt down beside her. I saw a dark red bruise already forming just below her hairline.

But she's alive, I saw gratefully.

Now what?

My heart pounded. The room tilted again, and I lost my balance.

I rubbed my forehead. Blinked, trying to make the room stand still.

I suddenly felt so hot. Burning hot. My face. My neck. My entire body.

As if a raging fever had swept over me. Like those rivers of red-hot molten lava you see in films about volcanoes.

I trembled from the heat. I struggled to climb to my feet. But the room danced around me. And the waves of heat—rising all around—made me so dizzy.

My head . . . swimming . . . swimming . . .

Sometimes when you have a high fever, you see crazy things. Bright colors. Strange objects.

And you think crazy thoughts. You believe you're okay, that you're thinking clearly. But your thoughts are wild. Totally insane.

I think that's what happened to me.

I think that's what the fever did to me.

Because as I struggled to steady the spinning, tilting room . . . as I struggled to stop the loud throbbing of my heart . . . to stop trembling . . . sweating . . . shaking all over from the raging heat . . . As I struggled to think clearly, I acted.

I moved.

I acted without thinking. Without even realizing what I was doing.

And when my mind finally cleared, I saw what I had done. I had tied Eden's arms behind her back. Tied her ankles together.

I had tied her up with bath towels. Bath towels rolled up, rolled tightly. I had tied up my friend and taped her mouth shut with strip after strip of masking tape.

I had pulled her to a sitting position.

Her eyes were open now. She looked up at me groggily. Struggled to speak but could only grunt.

She stared at me, raising her eyebrows in disbelief. Questioning me.

What are you doing, Hope? What are you going to do to me?

Silent questions I couldn't answer.

Because I *didn't know* what I was doing.

Gripped by the sudden fever. Gripped by my desperate desire to protect the only boy who ever cared for me.

Gripped by some crazy, invisible force, I didn't know what I was doing. Or what I was about to do.

But I bent over Eden. Slid my hands under her armpits. And pulled her.

Pulled her over the carpet.

She squirmed and tried to kick me. But I had tied her tightly. She couldn't free herself. She couldn't get away.

I pulled with all my strength. Dragged her. Dragged her . . .

She tried to hold back. But her body slid over the carpet.

"I'm not going to hurt you!" I gasped. My voice came out so high and shrill.

"Mmmmmm! Mmmmmmppppf!" she tried to protest. She tried to shout at me through the layers of masking tape.

I dragged her across the room. Past the bunkbed that belonged to Angel and Jasmine.

It's so lucky they had early classes, I thought.

And then I thought: If they were here in the room, would I be doing this? What *would* I be doing?

Eden kicked out both legs. She tried to dig her heels into the carpet.

But I dragged her past the bunkbed. Into the clothes closet against the back wall.

"Mmmmmppp! Mmmmmmmppph!"

I shut the door so I wouldn't have to hear her muffled cries. I slammed the door hard. And leaned back against the wall, gasping for breath. My heart pounding . . . pounding so hard, I thought it might burst.

My mouth felt so dry. My throat ached. Every muscle in my body quivered.

I wiped sweat off my forehead with the sleeve of my nightshirt. Took deep breaths. Slower. Slower.

Waited for my breathing to return to normal. And listened.

Could I hear Eden's gagged protests through the closet door? Could I hear the thud of her feet kicking the closet floor?

No.

Silence in the room now. Silence except for my wheezing breaths.

Now what? I asked myself.

What do I do now?

The fever had gone down. The heat had evaporated. Slipped away. I began to see clearly again.

And to think clearly.

Now what? Now what?

I can't hide her in the closet forever.

What will I tell Angel and Jasmine?

Why did I do this? What was I thinking?

Maybe I should tell Darryl what I've done, I decided. Maybe he will have an idea of what to do next.

"No!" I cried out loud. "No!" I tugged the sides of my hair with both hands.

Darryl will only want to kill her.

Darryl thinks killing is the solution to all his problems. He has no other ideas.

And I can't allow that. I can't. Eden is my friend, after all. One of my best friends.

So I can't tell Darryl. And I can't tell Angel and Jasmine.

So what can I do?

I shut my eyes, struggling to think clearly.

A sound across the room made me open them.

"Huh?" I stared at the figure in the open doorway.

Melanie.

Melanie staring across the room at me; her mouth open, her eyes wide.

How long had she been there? How much had she seen?

chapter

23

"The—the door was open," Melanie stammered.

"Oh." I stood up straight, pulling down my night-shirt. I could feel my face growing hot, and I knew I was blushing.

Had she seen me drag Eden into the closet? Had she?

I brushed my hair back from my forehead. It was matted down with sweat. "Hot in here," I muttered.

Melanie narrowed her eyes at me. "Are you okay?" she asked.

"It's just so . . . hot," I replied. "I don't know. Maybe I have a temperature or something."

I turned my gaze to the closet door. Had I closed it all the way?

How long had Melanie been standing there? Would I have to drag *her* into the closet too?

Crazy question. But I still wasn't thinking clearly. I still hadn't caught my balance.

"What do you want?" I blurted out. It sounded more hostile than I'd planned. "I mean . . . it's kind of a busy morning," I added. "I . . . overslept and—"

"I just wanted to remind you about the dorm meeting tonight," Melanie replied, still eyeing me suspiciously. "We're going to try to get some answers about campus safety."

"Good," I muttered.

Melanie shook her head. "Two murders. Two kids killed so viciously," she said with emotion. "It's so awful. Can you imagine what their parents must be going through?"

"No," I replied in a whisper, lowering my eyes. "I can't imagine."

"I—I'm scared to walk across The Triangle at night," Melanie confessed. She shuddered. Her dark bangs shuddered with her.

She wore a navy-blue wool sweater pulled down over black leggings. She looked as perfect as ever.

I brushed my hair back with my hands again. I knew I looked as if a hurricane had blown over me.

"Anyway, we hope to get some answers tonight," she said. "The dean promised to come. And someone from the local police. And the director of campus security."

"That's good," I repeated awkwardly.

"It's at seven tonight. Downstairs in the lobby," she told me.

"Okay. I'll be there," I replied. "I—I hope they catch the guy soon. We're all total wrecks here."

Again, she narrowed her eyes at me. "Are you sure you're okay, Hope?"

I nodded. "Yeah. Sure. Just fine. I just have to get cleaned up," I told her. "I'm off to a late start."

I pulled open the room door and held it for her, hoping she'd take the hint.

"Okay. See you later," she said. She forced a smile and made her way out.

Melanie is very suspicious, I realized as I closed the door behind her. She kept studying me, watching my every move.

What has she heard? What has she seen?

Maybe she saw Darryl sneaking in and out of my room, I decided. Maybe she thinks I'm hiding him now.

Darryl. I've got to talk to him. If Melanie suspects . . .

Darryl has to go away for a while, I decided.

It will break my heart. But he has to leave the campus. Get far away. Hide somewhere safe until this all blows over.

Yes. I suddenly started to feel better.

I realized that I'd finally had a good idea. The right idea.

Darryl had to go away.

But will he agree? I wondered. What will he say when I tell him?

Will he rant and roar and get furious as usual? Will he try to argue with me? Will he tell me that he'll never leave me—never?

Or will he realize that this is the best plan? Will he see that I'm only thinking of his safety? Only thinking of *our* future?

Outside the window, clouds rolled away from the sun. Orange morning sunlight washed into the room.

I moved to the window and felt the warmth of the sunlight on my face. Squinting down at the campus below, I saw dark-uniformed figures scurrying around.

Police officers!

What's going on? I wondered.

I peered through the glare on the glass. And saw three officers surrounding a guy with dark hair.

Darryl?

Yes. Darryl.

"Oh no!" I cried, pressing my hands against the glass.

What are they *doing* to him?

I pressed my face against the glass and squinted into the sun. One officer grabbed Darryl's shoulder. The other two moved on either side.

Are they arresting him? I wondered.

Do they know? Do they know he's the one?

I have to get out there, I decided. I have to try to help Darryl.

Maybe I can give him an alibi. Maybe I can persuade the cops that Darryl was with me when the murders occurred.

I have to try, I told myself.

I can't just stand here watching. Watching them take Darryl away.

My heart pounding, I crossed the room. Pulled open the door. Started into the hall—before I realized I was still in my nightshirt.

Down the hall, two girls looked up.

I spun around and darted back into the room.

"Got to get dressed. Got to hurry," I told myself.

I had to get outside before the police dragged Darryl away.

I ran to the closet to get some clothes. I grabbed the handle, started to turn it—and remembered Eden.

Eden. My prisoner.

My friend. My prisoner.

A sick cry escaped my throat.

How could I have done that to her? Was I out of my head? Was I totally nuts?

I'll let her out, I decided. I'll explain to her. I'll apologize and beg her to forgive me.

Eden will understand. Maybe . . .

I took a deep breath and pulled open the closet door. "Eden—?"

She was gone.

chapter

24

I stared down at the closet floor. At a crumpled pair of jeans on the floor. And a pair of black sneakers on their sides.

"Eden—?"

The closet darkened in front of me, as if a black cloud were sweeping over it. I felt myself pulled, pulled into the gaping darkness.

As if the closet were opening wide, revealing a black hole at its back. Opening wide and swallowing me whole. Sucking me into endless darkness.

"Eden—?"

Where was she? Where?

I heard a soft groan. Behind me.

"Huh?"

I spun around. Blinked twice. Three times.

Eden rolled over in her bed. She raised her head off the pillow and opened one eye. "What time is it?" she asked sleepily. "Is it late?"

I was too stunned to answer. I grabbed the sides of the closet with both hands. My mouth dropped open.

Eden opened her other eye. "Hope—are you okay?"

"N-no," I choked out.

I felt the closet pulling me inside. Swallowing me. Swallowing me whole. Felt the blackness sweep over me. So cold . . .

"No!" I repeated.

I pushed myself away from the closet. Stumbled out into the light.

I staggered halfway across the room, unable to breathe. Unable to think.

"Eden?"

She squinted up from her bed, still half asleep. "What's happening, Hope?" she asked.

"You're not in the closet," I murmured.

Her expression changed to confusion. She pulled herself up to a sitting position. "Excuse me?"

I dropped down beside her on the bed. I felt so happy and so frightened at the same time.

Happy that Eden was okay. Happy that she wasn't tied up in the closet.

Frightened about myself, about my mind.

Am I going crazy? Am I totally losing it?

I knew I hadn't dreamed that I hit Eden over the head and tied her up. It was no dream. I'd been wide awake.

So had I *imagined* it all?

How could I imagine something so vividly? I wondered. How could something I imagined seem so *real?*

I shut my eyes tight and buried my head in my hands.

I didn't want to think about this. I wanted everything to disappear.

I wanted to wake up and have everything nice again.

"Oh!" I jumped up, suddenly remembering Darryl. Darryl surrounded by three policemen.

I had to get dressed. I had to get outside and help him.

Darryl. Poor Darryl.

"Hope—what's wrong?" Eden demanded. "What *is* it?"

I didn't answer her. My head spun. My legs felt rubbery and weak. But I ran to the window and peered down at the campus.

And saw Darryl. By himself now.

No cops. The officers had left.

And Darryl stood alone. Staring up at me. Staring up at my window.

With the most terrifying look of pure hatred on his face.

part five

Jasmine

chapter

25

I jogged across Pine Street and crossed without looking, ignoring the red light. A car honked, but I didn't stop to see what the problem was.

The neon sign in the front of the Campus Corner came into view in the middle of the next block. I ducked my head into the swirling, cold wind and began to run full speed.

I was late for work. And I knew Marty would be in my face the moment I stepped through the glass door.

"Jasmine—where have you been?"

"Jasmine—you know you're the only waitress on duty after four. How can you stand me up like this?"

"Jasmine—didn't *anyone* teach you about responsibility?"

I've heard it all before. I've heard him shout and curse and threaten to fire me.

I try to get to work on time. And I try to be the best waitress I can be, even though it's boring, lonely work.

But sometimes the time goes by and I don't realize it. Sometimes I get involved in something more important and don't want to admit that I have no choice. That I have to keep this job if I want to stay at Ivy State.

Anyway, I burst breathlessly into the restaurant. And started to pull back my long blond hair. Marty makes all of us wear hair nets, which I really hate. *He* doesn't wear one—and he's the cook!

I tugged off my parka and tossed it over a coat hook. And started to the kitchen behind the lunch counter to get my apron.

Mrs. Jacklin, my daily customer, was lowering herself into her usual table. I glanced at the coffeepot to make sure there was coffee. Mrs. Jacklin, I knew, would be lingering over her cup of coffee for at least an hour.

My eyes swept the restaurant. A couple of guys from the college sat at a back booth with slices of pie and Cokes. No one else.

Marty was sitting on a wooden stool near the sink, reading a magazine. He raised his eyes when I came in, and his expression turned sour.

"Jasmine, I have to talk to you," he said quietly. His cheeks turned red. He rolled up the magazine between his hands and slapped his lap with it.

"Sorry I'm late," I murmured, reaching for my apron.

"I really need a waitress here at four," Marty said. He glanced at the clock above the sink. Four-twenty.

"That clock is fast," I said, avoiding his eyes.

"I'm very disappointed in you," he said, tossing the rolled-up magazine onto the counter.

"Sorry," I muttered. What else could I say?

"I know you're a bright girl," Marty continued, frowning at me. "Sure, you're quiet. Not much personality . . ."

You don't have to insult me because I'm a few minutes late! I thought angrily. But I let it pass.

"But I expected you to be more responsible," he continued.

How long is he going to scold me? I wondered. I already said I was sorry.

"I—I have to get Mrs. Jacklin her coffee," I stammered.

Marty shook his head. "No, you don't. I'll get it. You stay here."

He slid off the stool. Disappeared into the front for a few seconds. I heard the clink of coffee cups. Heard him say something to Mrs. Jacklin.

When he returned to the kitchen, his cheeks reddened again. He shut the kitchen door.

Uh-oh, I thought. This looks like bad news.

"I'm afraid I have to let you go," he said. "I'm really sorry, Jasmine."

"Oh, wait. Please—" I started. I really didn't want

to lose this job. "I won't be late again, Mr. Dell. I promise."

I sounded like a five-year-old. But I didn't care.

Marty shook his head. "Being late is one thing, Jasmine," he replied quietly. "But where were you yesterday?"

"Excuse me?" My mouth dropped open.

"You didn't show up at all yesterday," he said, sighing. He picked up the magazine and rolled it tensely between his hands. "I had to run the place myself. And we were really busy."

"Yesterday?" I repeated. I suddenly felt sick. My legs felt weak. My throat tightened.

"Yes. Where were you?" he demanded.

I stared at him. "Uh . . ." I thought hard. Where was I yesterday afternoon? Where?

"I don't remember," I told him.

His face twisted in disgust. "You don't even have an excuse? That's the best you can do? *You don't remember?* Why don't you tell me you were sick? Or that you had to take a test? Give me a good excuse, Jasmine."

I shook my head. I felt dizzy. "But . . . really," I insisted. "I really don't remember *where* I was yesterday afternoon." I swallowed hard. "In fact, I don't remember *anything* about yesterday," I gasped. "Nothing at all."

Marty sighed. He took the apron from my hands. "Here. I've written you a check for what I owe you."

I took the check from him without looking at it. The kitchen blurred. I was concentrating . . . concentrating on yesterday.

Where was I? Where?

I had to get out of that kitchen. I had to go somewhere and think.

"Good-bye, Jasmine," Marty said, slapping the magazine nervously against his leg. "I'm sorry it didn't work out. I really am."

I mumbled something to him. I didn't even hear myself.

Then I floated back out to the restaurant to get my parka. Mrs. Jacklin offered a greeting as I passed her table. But I didn't reply.

I pulled the parka off the hook and stepped outside without putting it on.

"Where was I yesterday?" I asked myself out loud.

Why can't I remember?

What's wrong with me?

chapter
_____
26

 I n a frightened daze, I wandered across the campus. Past dark-uniformed police officers and groups of students huddled together, talking excitedly.

I found a table at the back of the cafeteria in the Student Union, and sat down with a cup of coffee and a sweet roll. Sat down to think. To remember.

Start somewhere, I instructed myself. Just try to remember *something*.

I took a long sip of coffee. Strong and bitter. Just what I needed to wake up my brain.

I remembered Hope being upset about something. Yes. I was asleep, my covers pulled up to my head. And Hope was upset because something terrible had happened.

Again.

Keep thinking, I ordered myself. *It's coming back to you.*

But before I could remember more, someone plopped down across from me at my table. I saw a dark, plaid shirt. Straight dark hair, unbrushed and wild. Pale blue eyes. Eyes that stared coldly and didn't blink.

"Darryl—!"

I scraped my chair back. Started to get up.

He tugged my arm. "Don't get tense, Jasmine. I just want to sit down a minute. I just want to talk."

I pulled my arm free and dropped back into my chair. I didn't want to sit with Darryl. He frightened me. Those cold eyes frightened me.

I never understood how Hope could be so devoted to him. I thought of him as a time bomb. He always seemed ready to explode.

And when he did, someone always got hurt.

"What's wrong?" I asked, gripping my coffee cup with both hands. "What's going on? There are cops all over the campus."

He rolled his eyes. "Tell me about it," he muttered. He pulled up the collar of his flannel shirt, as if he were cold.

I sipped the coffee. I hoped he didn't see my hand tremble as I lifted the cup.

He really frightened me.

"Three cops stopped me," he continued, shaking his head. "I was on my way to see Hope, and they stopped me. And questioned me. About that guy who got murdered. You know. At the driving range."

I *didn't* know about it. Did it happen yesterday? I wondered. Did it happen during the time I can't remember?

I glanced over Darryl's shoulder and saw Margie a few tables down. She was with a bunch of girls I didn't recognize. For some reason, she was staring hard at me.

When I stared back, she turned away.

What's *her* problem? I wondered.

"Hope wants me to leave." Darryl's voice broke into my thoughts.

I turned back to him. "Excuse me?"

"Hope wants me to leave," he repeated impatiently. "She wants me to go hide for a while."

I struggled to make sense of his words. I couldn't believe Hope would let him go away. She needed him close to her. She needed him so badly.

"What—what did you tell her?" I stammered. As I reached for the coffee cup, my hand brushed over the sweet roll. I realized I hadn't touched it.

"I said *no way!*" Darryl declared angrily. His eyes flared. I saw him ball his hands into fists.

I shrank back. Was he going to take out his anger on *me?*

"I'm not running away," he shouted.

Again, I saw Margie staring at me from across the cafeteria.

"I'm not going anywhere," Darryl repeated.

"That's what I told Hope." He rolled his eyes again. "Like I need her advice? I don't need her advice."

"So what did *she* say when you refused to go hide somewhere?" I asked.

Darryl lowered his eyes to the floor. He drummed his fingers on the tabletop.

"What did Hope say?" I repeated.

"We . . . argued," Darryl murmured, still avoiding my eyes. "We fought about it."

I felt a sudden stab of fear. "And?"

When he raised his eyes to me, his face was pale. His chin trembled. He swept his hair off his forehead. "We fought and I—I did something terrible."

"Oh *no!*" I gasped.

He nodded. His eyes watered over. "I hurt her, Jasmine. I hurt her real bad."

part six

Hope

chapter

27

I almost never cry. Some girls I know cry all the time. They cry when they mess up an exam. They cry when a guy stands them up. They cry when they break a nail.

But I'm not much of a crier. I guess it's because I cried so much when I was a little girl. I cried until I realized how much my mother enjoyed seeing me cry.

Then I stopped. And I haven't cried since.

But today I was hunched on the edge of my bed, mopping my tear-drenched cheeks when Jasmine came bursting into the dorm room.

No way I could hide the fact that I'd been crying. My eyes were red-rimmed and watery. My cheeks were red and swollen. My T-shirt was soaked.

"Hope—?" Jasmine's eyes bulged and she raised a

hand to her mouth. "What *happened?*" she cried. "Are you okay?"

I nodded, brushing wet strands of hair from my face. "Yeah. I guess."

"What did he *do* to you?" Jasmine dropped beside me on the bed and wrapped an arm around my waist. "What did he do?"

I blinked a few times. "How did you know it was Darryl?" I asked, my voice still shaky from all that crying, my throat raw.

"I—I ran into him. At the cafeteria," Jasmine replied, holding me. "He seemed really messed up. He told me he hurt you."

I sucked in a deep breath. "Yes. He hurt me. He hurt my feelings."

She reacted with surprise. "Your feelings? You mean—he didn't hit you or anything?"

I didn't want to scream or cry anymore. But I couldn't hold in my pain. "No. He didn't hit me. He did much worse, Jasmine. *He called me names!*" I wailed.

Jasmine's mouth dropped open.

"He called me horrible names!" I cried shrilly, letting the tears flow again. They rolled down my hot cheeks like a river. "He said I was fat. He called me a cow. He's never done that before, Jasmine! Never! I—I was so hurt!"

"But—but—" Jasmine sputtered. "At least he didn't—"

"I'd rather be hit!" I cried, pushing her away. "I'd

rather be slugged unconscious than be called horrible names by him!"

"But why was he so angry at you, Hope?" she demanded.

"Because I tried to send him away," I sobbed. "I told him he had to go somewhere far away. And stay there. It was only for his own good. But he thought— he thought . . ."

"He thought you were breaking up with him?" Jasmine asked.

"I . . . I guess," I choked out. I covered my face with both hands. My skin felt wet and puffy and gross.

Jasmine tsk-tsked. "What a mess," she murmured.

"I'm so worried for him," I told her. "I've never seen him so out of control. He won't listen to me. He won't listen to someone who only wants to help him. I don't know what he'll do next."

I took a deep breath. I forced myself to stop crying. Enough tears, I told myself. They aren't helping anyway.

I climbed shakily to my feet. And glanced at the desk clock.

"The meeting," I murmured.

Jasmine narrowed her eyes at me. "Meeting?"

"The dorm meeting," I replied. "About safety. About what to do about the murders." I let out a bitter sigh. "I could tell them what to do about the murders. I know *exactly* how to stop the murders— don't I?"

Jasmine nodded solemnly. "Yes. We all know how to stop the murders."

"How can I go sit in this stupid meeting and pretend not to know anything?" I asked her. "How can I sit there with all these frightened kids, knowing who the murderer is? Knowing that the murderer is someone I care about so much?"

"Maybe Eden is right," Jasmine replied in a whisper. "Maybe we have no choice, Hope. Maybe we have to call the police and tell them about Darryl."

"Ohhhh." I uttered a weary moan. I suddenly felt so tired, so sick and tired.

If only we could go back in time two weeks. If only we could put our lives in rewind. If we could back up two weeks, I could get to Darryl before he murdered Brendan. I could stop him. Stop him from killing Eden's friend Dave too.

And then we could all be happy again. And then we could all be *normal* again.

But why think about the impossible?

I had to stop daydreaming. And try to decide what to do in the real world. The world that suddenly had become so horrifying.

Shaking my head, I crossed to the closet and began to search for something to wear. I lifted out some sweaters. Then I shoved them back and slammed the closet door.

"I can't," I told Jasmine. "I can't go. No way. I— I'll just do something I'll regret."

Jasmine nodded solemnly but didn't reply.

I pictured Darryl. That sweet, serious face of his. And something inside me snapped.

I guess I was holding too much horror inside. It all just burst out of me.

I tilted my head back in a long, shrill scream. Not a human sound. But a desperate animal cry.

And then I tore past Jasmine, nearly knocking her down. I ran out the door and down the long dorm hall, crowded with girls on their way to the meeting.

"Hey—Hope!" I heard someone call. Melanie, I think.

I didn't turn back. I didn't stop running.

I leaped into the stairwell and headed down, taking two stairs at a time.

I heard voices calling me. Shouts of surprise.

My shoes clanged heavily against the concrete steps.

Down, down.

The gray walls a blur on both sides.

Where was I going?

I didn't know.

I just had to run.

I didn't realize that I would never spend another night in Fear Hall.

part seven

Angel

chapter
28

For the first few minutes, I let the guy kiss me. And then I wrapped my fingers around the back of his neck and kissed him back.

His lips pressed harder. His strong arms tightened around my waist.

After a few minutes more, he pulled his head back. He smiled and took a few deep breaths.

We were both breathing hard.

My heart was pounding. I could still taste his lips on mine. Salty and sweet at the same time.

"What's your name?" he asked, his arms still tight around me.

I leaned back against the hood of his car and gazed up at the moon. The cool night air felt so good on my hot face. The breeze fluttered my hair.

"Do you have a name?" he teased.

"Angel," I told him.

"Angel," he repeated. He trailed a finger gently down my cheek. "I like that name." His grin grew wider. "Are you feeling devilish tonight, Angel?"

I nuzzled my cheek against his. "Maybe," I whispered, smiling back at him.

We kissed again.

"What's *your* name?" I asked breathlessly, when we finally pulled apart.

"Billy Joe," he replied, adjusting the sleeve of his Ivy State sweatshirt. "But everyone calls me B.J."

I snickered. "Are you from Texas, B.J.? Guys from Texas are always called B.J. or T.J. or something."

"Oklahoma," he said softly. His expression hardened. I saw that he didn't like to be teased.

I playfully messed up his curly, blond hair.

"Hey—" He pulled my hand away.

I turned when I heard a car door slam nearby.

B.J. and I were in a parking lot behind a row of stores in town. The dark lot stood empty. The car I heard must be on the street, I realized.

I snuggled against him. He felt so warm and smelled so good. I felt so happy to get away from the campus for a short while. To get away from all the frightened students.

All the frantic talk about the murders.

All the fear. The cold fear.

"Do you always pick up guys like this?" B.J. asked, grinning. He reached up and smoothed my straight, blond hair off my face.

"Yes. Always," I teased.

He laughed. "And they named you *Angel?*"

I pushed him back and stepped away from the car. "I just liked you," I told him. "Something about your smile, I guess."

I had stopped in that coffee bar off campus because I didn't know where else to go. I didn't want to go back to the dorm. And I didn't want to hang out at the Student Union or the library.

So I popped into the coffee bar—Java Jim's. And I was ordering a small coffee at the counter when I saw B.J. standing at a small table by the window. Staring at me. Smiling at me.

The next thing I knew, we were leaning against his old Toyota, kissing in the parking lot behind the coffee bar.

I needed him there tonight, I realized.

I needed someone to hold me. Someone to make me feel happy.

Someone to make me forget everything I knew about the ugly murders on campus.

Okay. It's true.

I do this a lot. I find guys in restaurants and movie theaters and stores. And I end up in dark parking lots with them.

But what's the harm in it?

What's the harm in a little warmth, a little happiness?

Hope understands. She knows that sometimes you cannot control everything you do every moment. Sometimes you have to give in to your feelings.

Eden says I live in a fantasy world.

But what's so terrible about that?

I snuggled against B.J. "Where do you live?" I whispered. "In a dorm?"

"No. In an old apartment north of campus," he replied. He wrapped his arms around my waist again. "I'd show it to you, but . . . I have two roommates."

"That's okay. I like it here," I replied. "Very cozy."

We kissed again.

And as we kissed, I heard a scraping sound. Like shoes over concrete.

I opened my eyes. And saw a dark figure jogging across the parking lot. His body bent forward, hands pumping at his sides.

I jerked my face away from B.J.'s.

"Darryl—!" I choked out. "What are you *doing* here?"

"Huh?" B.J. spun around so fast, he nearly stumbled.

Darryl stood stiffly, legs apart, hands balled into fists at his sides. As if expecting trouble.

As if ready to fight.

"Darryl—why did you follow me?" I cried, grabbing B.J.'s sweatshirt sleeve. Squeezing it. Squeezing it.

Darryl didn't say a word. He glared furiously, first at B.J., then at me.

B.J. tugged his sleeve free and stared at me. "Angel—what's going on here?" he demanded.

I kept my eyes on Darryl. I watched his entire body tense. Saw him slowly raise his fists.

"Darryl—you have no business here," I shouted. "Go away—now! I mean it!"

Darryl didn't budge. He didn't speak. He didn't blink.

"I—I don't like this, Angel," B.J. stammered, backing away. I saw a glint of fear in his eyes.

"Darryl—get away!" I shrieked. "You have no right! You have no right to follow me—to spy on me! What do you think you're doing?"

Darryl scowled and spit on the concrete. He took a menacing step toward B.J. and me.

"What's going on?" B.J. demanded again. "Angel, I don't like this. You're frightening me. You really are."

Darryl uttered a nasty laugh. He raised his fists, his eyes narrowed at B.J.

"No—!" I shrieked. "Don't hurt him, Darryl! I'm warning you—don't hurt him!"

"I'm sorry," B.J. murmured. "You're really scaring me."

He pushed past me. Jerked open the car door. Dove behind the wheel. Slammed the door behind him.

"No—let me in!" I wailed. "B.J.—don't leave me here with him!"

Darryl tossed back his head and laughed.

"B.J.—please!" I screamed. "Don't leave me!"

I pounded on the car window. Pounded with both fists.

But the car roared away. I had to jump back to keep my feet from being run over.

"B.J.—please! Please!"

The car jumped the curb. Bounced out of the parking lot. And squealed away.

I turned, trembling, to face Darryl. "Now what?" I whispered. "What are you going to do to me?"

part eight

Hope

chapter

29

I returned to the dorm at about eleven, feeling dazed and exhausted. I stepped into the elevator, pressed thirteen—and heard someone say my name.

"Hope—!"

I turned to see Melanie at the back of the elevator. She was lugging an enormous bag of laundry. I guessed she was on her way up from the basement laundry room.

"Hope, I didn't see you at the dorm meeting," she scolded.

I raised my eyes to the flashing floor numbers above the door. "Yeah. I know," I replied. "I—I had to go out."

"It was a good meeting," Melanie said. "I think we

got our feelings across to the dean and the security people."

"That's good," I muttered.

Why was it taking the elevator so long? I really didn't want to chat with Melanie about campus safety precautions.

"They promised to put extra guards on duty," Melanie reported. "Starting tomorrow."

She shifted the big laundry bag to her other hand. "A lot of kids are still frightened, though," she continued. "No one is going out at night. It's amazing. The Triangle is like a ghost town after eight o'clock."

I shook my head. "Terrible," I murmured. I raised my eyes to the floor numbers. Eight . . . nine . . .

"Do they have any idea who the murderer is?" I asked, trying to sound sincere. "Any idea at all? Is it some wacko crazy person?"

Melanie swallowed. "They don't have a clue," she replied softly. "That's what's so frightening, don't you think? They don't know where to begin to find the guy. He—he could be anywhere. He could be hiding somewhere on campus right now."

I pretended to shudder. "Sorry I missed the meeting," I murmured. I held the door open for her. She dragged the laundry bag with both hands.

"It felt good to do laundry," she said as I followed her down the long hall. "You know. Making something clean and nice. It helped me forget about the murders for a short while."

I didn't know how to reply. I *couldn't* forget about

146

the murders for *any* while. I couldn't think about anything else.

I'd been wandering around all night in a fog, unable to think, unable to decide what to do.

I've got to talk to my roommates, I decided. I've got to call a meeting of our own.

I want to hear what Angel, Jasmine, and Eden have to say. I need to hear how they feel now. About Darryl. About turning him in.

I can't go on like this, I knew.

I can't keep this horrible secret inside much longer.

If the others vote to call the police, I won't stop them. I'll let them turn Darryl in.

It will break my heart. But I won't stop them.

I took a deep breath. Pushed open the door to 13-B. And stepped inside.

chapter

30

The room stood dark and empty. I clicked on all the lights. Then I opened both windows to let in fresh air. I checked the fire escape outside the back window. I guess I was making sure Darryl wasn't hiding out there.

You're getting paranoid, Hope, I scolded myself. Why would Darryl hide from *you?*

Feeling tense and upset and a little frantic, I went into the bathroom and took a long shower.

The warm water felt so refreshing. I need to feel clean. To wash away the feeling of guilt I had. To wash away my dirty secret about Darryl.

After the shower, I put on a clean sweater over a clean pair of jeans. I took a long time brushing my hair, gazing at myself in the mirror. Thinking . . . thinking hard about what had to be done.

My three roommates appeared a few minutes later. Angel came in with her lipstick smeared, eye makeup staining her cheeks.

"Where were *you?*" I demanded.

She shrugged. "Nowhere really. Just out." Then she added, "I met a guy."

"So what else is new?" Eden chimed in, rolling her eyes.

Jasmine didn't say anything. She sat on the edge of her bed and fiddled tensely with a strand of her blond hair.

"That creep Darryl followed me," Angel said, scowling. She caught her reflection in the dresser mirror. She started to rub the eye makeup off her cheeks with a tissue.

I took a deep breath. "We have to talk about Darryl," I said. I pulled out the desk chair and sat on it backward, facing my three friends.

"Yes. We do," Angel agreed. "He's out of control, Hope. It has to stop."

I gripped the back of the desk chair with both hands. "What do you think we should do?" I asked.

All three of them began talking at once.

"Right from the start, I said we have to call the police," Eden said. "I know it's hard for you, Hope."

"We all know how hard it is," Angel agreed. "But he's killed two kids. And he's following us everywhere."

"He'll kill again," Jasmine offered in a tiny voice. "We don't want to be responsible for that."

"She's right," Eden said heatedly. "If someone else dies because of Darryl, it will be our fault. We will be just as guilty as he is. Because we didn't turn him in."

I swallowed hard. They all agreed on what we should do. They all agreed that we should tell the police what we knew.

But could I do it?

Could I really go to the phone and turn in the person I cared the most about in the whole world?

"Maybe I could talk to him," I suggested, one last desperate attempt to save him. "Maybe I could convince him to go get the help he needs."

Eden sighed. "They don't call you Hope for nothing," she said, shaking her head.

"He won't listen to you," Angel said softly. "You know he won't, Hope. He never does. If you try to talk to him, he'll only get angry again."

"You remember the last time you tried to help him," Eden added. "He yelled at you—didn't he? He called you horrible names."

Yes. Yes, he did.

Her words brought it back. I saw Darryl's anger again. Heard him say those ugly things to me. Saw him staring up at my dorm window with such hatred on his face. And felt the hurt all over again.

"If you try to help him," Eden continued. "There's no telling *what* he will do."

"He's so dangerous," Jasmine murmured. She shuddered.

I heard a sound in the hall. With a gasp, I turned to the door, expecting Darryl to come bursting in.

But it was just someone walking past our room.

I took a deep breath. My mouth suddenly felt so dry. "Okay," I whispered. "We can't live in fear like this. Wondering what horrible thing Darryl will do next. Who he will hurt. Who he will *kill.*"

I gripped the back of the chair tighter, so tight my hands ached. "Okay. Okay. Okay. Okay," I chanted. "We have to call the police. We have to end this nightmare."

I raised my eyes to the phone. It was only a few feet away on the desktop. But I realized I couldn't get over there.

I couldn't be the one to turn Darryl in.

"Eden—will you make the call?" I asked.

She nodded grimly. "Okay." She climbed up from her chair and strode quickly to the phone. "Okay, Hope. I'll do it."

She picked up the receiver.

And someone pounded hard on our door.

chapter

31

*J*asmine let out a shriek. Eden gripped the receiver and spun to the door. I jumped to my feet.

"Who—who is it?" I tried to call, but my voice came out in a choked whisper.

"It isn't Darryl," Eden said, frowning. "He never knocks. He just barges in."

She was right. I took a deep breath and crossed to the door. I pulled it open a crack.

And stared at Ollie, the night guard.

"Is there a problem?" I asked.

"A young man left this," Ollie replied. He held up a jacket. Angel's jacket. "Is it yours? He said a blond girl left it in his car."

So Angel had been with some guy in a car, I

realized. Probably making out in a parking lot, knowing Angel.

"It's my roommate's jacket." I took the jacket from Ollie. "Thanks a lot. I'll give it to her," I said.

He nodded his bald head and started back to the elevator.

I closed the door behind me and turned back to my roommates. Eden was already talking into the phone.

I tossed the jacket to Angel. "You forgot this," I told her.

"Sshhhh." Eden raised a finger to her lips. "I'm talking to a police sergeant."

I stepped up beside her, my heart suddenly pounding.

Were we doing the right thing?

Yes. Finally. We were finally doing what we should have done a long time ago.

Poor Darryl . . .

My poor baby . . .

"Yes. I'm in room 13-B," Eden was telling the officer. "Roommates? Yes. I have three roommates." She told him our names.

"The boy's name is Darryl Hoode," Eden continued. She glanced up at me. "He lives downstairs in Fear Hall," she reported. "Yes. On the boys' floor."

I heard a rattling at the back window. The wind shaking the fire escape railings.

"Please hurry," Eden was saying to the officer. "We—we don't know where Darryl is right now. But he's really dangerous. Please—we're very scared. All four of us—we're so scared."

She hung up the phone and turned back to us. Her chin was trembling. Her face pale.

"I—I did it," she uttered.

"What did he say?" I demanded breathlessly. "Did he say they were sending someone?"

Eden nodded. "He said to lock our room door," she reported. "He said not to open it for anyone—until the officers arrive."

"But—it doesn't lock!" Jasmine cried. "The lock is broken!"

"Don't panic. They'll be here in ten minutes," Eden replied. "We should be okay, Jasmine. We should—"

She stopped with her mouth open as we heard more rattling at the back window.

We all turned—and saw Darryl climb in from the fire escape.

"What's up?" he asked.

chapter

32

"Darryl—what were you doing out there?" I demanded. I tried to sound calm. Normal. I didn't want to raise his suspicions.

A strange grin spread over his face. "Never mind that," he replied. "What were *you* doing in here?"

"I—I don't know what you mean," I stammered.

He took a few steps into the room. And turned to Eden. "Hi, Eden," he said with exaggerated warmth. "How's it going?"

Eden shrank back as Darryl moved toward her. "What's your problem?" she demanded.

"Like to talk on the phone?" Darryl asked. His smile faded. His eyes narrowed angrily.

"Leave Eden alone, Darryl," I warned. I tried to sound firm, but my voice trembled.

"Like to talk on the phone, Eden?" Darryl repeated, moving steadily toward her. Forcing her back. Back to the window. "Like to tell stories about me on the phone?"

"Darryl—wait!" Eden cried.

"Did you think I didn't hear you?" Darryl screamed, suddenly in a rage. "Did you think I wasn't out there the whole time? Did you think I wouldn't know what you were trying to do?"

"Darryl—get back!" I cried. "Don't touch Eden! We all decided—"

He let out a furious roar.

Eden raised her hands to shield herself.

"How *could* you?" Darryl roared. "How could you turn me in to the police?"

"Darryl—we decided we had no choice," I choked out. "We can't let you—"

I didn't get the rest of my words out.

Instead, I opened my mouth in a scream as Darryl grabbed Eden.

"Let her go! Let her go!" Angel shrieked.

Eden opened her mouth to scream.

But Darryl clamped a hand over it.

His other arm wrapped around her waist. He held her from behind.

"Let her go! Don't do it! *Don't!*" I wailed.

His eyes were wild. His mouth opened in a roar. He lifted Eden off the floor.

Lifted her. Lifted her.

Lifted her above his head with both hands as she squirmed and thrashed her arms and legs.

"Let her go!"

"Put her down!"

He lifted her higher. Held her above his head.

And then brought her down hard against his up-raised knee.

I heard a sickening *crack*.

"Ohhhhh." A moan of pain escaped Eden's throat.

He cracked her back, I realized.

He cracked her. Cracked her in two.

Her eyes rolled up in her head. Her head dropped and bounced against the floor.

And then, with a loud groan, Darryl lifted her again.

This time Eden didn't squirm or struggle. This time she hung limply in his arms.

He lifted her again. Lifted her. Her arms drooping down. Her mouth open. Eyes shut.

Lifted her. Lifted her.

And heaved her out the open window.

A second later, I heard a *thud* from the pavement below. Thirteen stories below.

"Nooooooo." A wail of horror burst from my lungs.

Jasmine was crying. Angel stared open-mouthed, frozen in place.

"Noooooooooo!"

I dove for Darryl. "You killed her! You killed Eden!" I shrieked.

I grabbed the front of his flannel shirt.

He glared at me, hunched over, panting like an animal. Like a wild animal.

Wild with fury, I tugged at his shirt with both hands. I reached up to scratch his face.

Missed.

He ducked away. Pulled free.

"You killed Eden! You killed Eden!" I cried.

Still panting, he nodded. His hair wild about his face. His eyes bulging. Sweat rolling off his forehead.

I dove for him again. I wanted to hurt him. I wanted to *kill* him.

He dodged away. Leaped onto the windowsill. Out the window.

Dropped onto the fire escape.

And vanished.

"He killed her. He killed her . . ." I repeated.

Jasmine cried, hands covering her face. Angel still hadn't moved.

A knock on the door.

And a voice called in, "Police!"

chapter

33

"Oh—!"

The officer pounded on the door.

I turned to the window. The room spun. The floor tilted up.

I saw Eden's horrified face again. And again I heard the sickening *crack* when Darryl snapped her back.

Jasmine and Angel were on their feet now, huddled together, arms around each other.

Their faces blurred in front of me. The room faded and threatened to go dark.

I'm going to faint, I realized.

"No—!"

I forced myself to remain standing.

I tried to move to the door—but something held me back.

Some kind of invisible force kept me from moving.

My fear? The horror I'd just seen?

I must have been in shock.

"Open up! Police!" the voice called in.

"Quick—" I whispered to Angel and Jasmine. "Quick—"

I started to the window.

I didn't know what I was doing. I had to be in shock. In total shock.

"Quick—" I repeated.

I lifted my knees onto the windowsill. And stared out at the night.

All a blur. The sky. The stars. The dark campus buildings all around.

A hazy blur.

I stumbled out onto the fire escape. "Hurry," I whispered.

And my two roommates joined me on the narrow, metal stairs.

We gripped the railing. Pressed our backs against the brick wall.

And listened as the door opened.

I peeked in and saw two blue-uniformed cops. Followed by Melanie.

They raised their eyes to the open window. I pulled back before they saw me.

My heart pounding, I pressed back against the wall and struggled to hear what they said.

"We got a call from a girl named Eden," the cop was telling Melanie.

"Huh?" I heard Melanie react with surprise. "What did she say her name was?"

"Eden," the cop repeated.

"Eden? I don't know any girl named Eden," Melanie replied. "Are you sure you got the name right?"

The policeman was silent for a moment. Then he said, "Yeah. Eden. She said she and her three roommates lived in 13-B."

Silence again.

Then Melanie said, "Roommates? She said she lived in 13-B and had roommates?"

"That's right," the policeman grunted.

"A girl named Hope lives in here, Officer," Melanie told him. "But, look—it's a single room. One bed—see? Hope doesn't have any roommates. She lives in here by herself."

chapter
34

I heard more footsteps. More voices.

I peeked into the room and saw Margie and Mary in the room. All three girls were talking at once. The two police officers had to ask them to be quiet.

"One at a time," a cop said impatiently. I saw him check his little writing pad. "What about Angel and Jasmine?" he asked the three girls.

They all shook their heads. "I don't know any girls with those names," Melanie said.

"Hope is kind of weird," Margie added. "She always seemed to be having loud arguments. Sometimes we'd hear her talking till late at night. But she's always alone in here."

"She works in a restaurant," Mary offered. "Campus Corner, off Pine Street. She's a waitress there

And once I saw her sitting in a booth, arguing with herself. Finally, the boss had to call her to the kitchen."

"Hmmmmm." I watched the cop write something on his pad.

"I saw Hope in the cafeteria the other day," Margie chimed in. "She was sitting there talking to herself. It was pretty weird."

"I've asked her if she's okay several times," Melanie told the cop. "I mean, I thought maybe she needed help. But she never wanted to talk to me."

Margie glanced toward the window. I pulled my head back.

"What about this boy, Darryl?" the other cop asked the three M's.

"Huh? Darryl?" Melanie replied. "I don't know anyone named Darryl. Does he go to Ivy State?"

"We were told he lives downstairs," the cop said. "On the boys' floor."

Margie and Mary let out startled laughs. "There aren't any boys in *this* dorm!" Mary cried.

"There *is* no boys' floor," Melanie agreed. "It's an all-girls dorm."

"Oh, wow!" Mary cried. "Do you think Hope made those other kids up? Did she imagine them?"

"Sounds like we have a loony," one of the cops said. "A dangerous loony."

"Maybe we've got a multiple personality here," his partner replied. "Do you think this Hope is all four girls? And Darryl too?"

"Maybe," the cop said softly. "The question is—did Hope cut up those two boys? Those boys aren't imaginary. Those two boys were real. And they were murdered by someone real."

"We'd better find her—fast," his partner said.

"I *knew* Hope was crazy!" I heard Margie exclaim.

"But can she really be a *killer?*" Melanie cried.

I didn't want to hear anymore.

I felt so angry—so *furious*—I wanted to dive back into the room and strangle Melanie and her two roommates with my bare hands.

How could they talk about me that way? How *could* they?

I pressed my back against the brick wall and turned to Angel and Jasmine. "They won't find us—will they, girls?" I whispered.

They both shook their heads.

"And by the time the police find us," I continued, "Melanie and her roommates will be dead. They will pay for calling us crazy. They will pay—right?"

"Right," Jasmine whispered.

"Right," Angel agreed.

"Right, Darryl?" I whispered. "We'll pay the three M's back—right, Darryl?"

He appeared beside me. He always appears when I want him to.

That's one reason I love him so much.

When I need him, I only have to think about him—and he magically appears.

"We'll pay them back—right, Darryl?" I repeated.

THE BEGINNING

"Right," Darryl whispered in my ear.

And then I heard a sharp cry from inside the room. And a policeman shouted, "There she is! On the fire escape! Catch her!"

TO BE CONTINUED . . .
DON'T MISS THE TERRIFYING ENDING, IN

FEAR HALL: THE CONCLUSION

About the Author

"Where do you get your ideas?"

That's the question that R.L. Stine is asked most often. "I don't know where my ideas come from," he says. "But I do know that I have a lot more scary stories in my mind that I can't wait to write."

So far, he has written over a hundred mysteries and thrillers for young people, all of them bestsellers.

Bob grew up in Columbus, Ohio. Today he lives in an apartment near Central Park in New York City with his wife, Jane, and son, Matt.

R.L. STINE'S GHOSTS OF FEAR STREET®

1	Hide and Shriek	52941-2/$3.99
2	Who's Been Sleeping in My Grave?	52942-0/$3.99
3	Attack of the Aqua Apes	52943-9/$3.99
4	Nightmare in 3-D	52944-7/$3.99
5	Stay Away From the Tree House	52945-5/$3.99
6	Eye of the Fortuneteller	52946-3/$3.99
7	Fright Knight	52947-1/$3.99
8	The Ooze	52948-X/$3.99
9	Revenge of the Shadow People	52949-8/$3.99
10	The Bugman Lives	52950-1/$3.99
11	The Boy Who Ate Fear Street	00183-3/$3.99
12	Night of the Werecat	00184-1/$3.99
13	How to be a Vampire	00185-X/$3.99
14	Body Switchers from Outer Space	00186-8/$3.99
15	Fright Christmas	00187-6/$3.99
16	Don't Ever get Sick at Granny's	00188-4/$3.99
17	House of a Thousand Screams	00190-6/$3.99
18	Camp Fear Ghouls	00191-4/$3.99
19	Three Evil Wishes	00189-2/$3.99
20	Spell of the Screaming Jokers	00192-2/$3.99
21	The Creature from Club Lagoona	00850-1/$3.99
22	Field of Screams	00851-X/$3.99

At the stroke of midnight...you are on Fear Street. Your footsteps echo as you walk past rows of houses. Houses with blank windows that seem to stare down at you. That seem to know your deepest, darkest secrets. Confide those secrets here...

R·L·STINE
FEAR STREET ®
Midnight Diary

Find out more about yourself, your friendships, your loves and your fears.

Take your first step onto Fear Street—if you dare.

Coming in mid-July

DEAR READERS:

Where will Hope go now that her secret has been revealed? Does she realize that her friends aren't real friends?

Does she know who the vicious killer really is? Are there more shocking surprises in store for her?

I know the answers to all those questions—because I wrote the book! I hope you will join me for the conclusion of FEAR HALL. I think it's one of my scariest finishes ever!

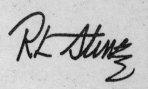

THE NIGHTMARES
NEVER END . . .
WHEN YOU VISIT

Turn the page to see
a terrifying sample of . . .

FEAR HALL: THE CONCLUSION
(Coming mid-July 1997)

Don't miss the shocking conclusion to
FEAR HALL: THE BEGINNING

Darryl's Revenge

I'm watching you, Mary.

I've been watching you for days. Following you from your dorm, Fear Hall—which used to be my home too. Following you to your classes.

I can't go to classes anymore, thanks to you. Thanks to you and your roommates. Since you talked to the police, I can't go to classes like the rest of you. I have to hide like a criminal.

Well, maybe I *am* a criminal, Mary. Maybe I'm a very dangerous criminal.

I guess you'll soon find out the truth.

Because I've been following you every day. I know your schedule by heart now. I know when you have classes and when you don't. I know where you eat lunch, and I know where you go to study.

And I know when you and Melanie go to the swim center for your team practices. I've been watching you swim. Yes, I have.

I've watched you practice all week. I've seen you work on your butterfly stroke. That's really a hard stroke, isn't it?

You've got to keep your head down, Mary. You've got to steady your breathing. That's what the coach has been telling you.

I could hear every word. You haven't seen me. But I've been watching you so closely.

I'm up here in the high balcony above the pool. Where the newspaper reporters sit. There's no one else up here during practices. I can watch you—and listen. And make my plans.

What a shame that you and your friends talked to the police, Mary. You got Hope in a lot of trouble. And now Hope is angry at me.

Hope blames me. She doesn't want me hanging around. She doesn't want to see poor Darryl anymore.

Hope and I were so close, Mary. So close.

And now she doesn't want to see me. Because she's in trouble. Thanks to you.

So I have to fix things. I have to win Hope back.

And I know just how to do it. I have to show Hope how much I care about her.

She would never pay you and your roommates back for what you did to her. But I will do it for her. And then Hope will know how much I care. She will know how much she needs me.

I'm watching you now, Mary. I'm sitting up here in the dark press room. Staring down at you through the long glass window.

Where is Melanie this afternoon? Why isn't she at practice today?

I can't believe she's going to miss your last swim. . . .

The coach squatted on the edge of the pool, her stopwatch raised in front of her face. She was timing the girls' laps, one by one.

Her whistle rang through the building, echoing off the tiled walls. The first swimmer dove into the pool with barely a splash.

Mary was fourth in line. I figured I had plenty of time.

I slid off my seat in the press box, backed away from the window, and made my way to the narrow stairway in back. I hurried down the curving stairs, leaning my weight on the railing to keep my steps as silent as possible.

A doorway opened into the pool area. I hesitated. Heard the coach's whistle, followed by another splash. Girls shouted encouragement to the new swimmer.

I followed the stairs down. I knew exactly where they led. I'd checked it all out carefully. I'd been running the plan through my head endlessly.

The doorway at the bottom of the steps led into the training room. I stopped at the closed door. I suddenly had a bad feeling.

Had someone locked the door?

That would ruin everything.

I turned the knob. The door opened easily. Breathing a silent sigh of relief, I slipped inside.

I glanced up and down the rows of lockers. I crept along the wall to the shower room and peered in. No one around.

I checked out the coach's little office across from the locker room. Sometimes people wait in there to see the coach after practice.

But today it was empty.

"Perfect," I murmured to myself.

The Jacuzzi bubbled and hissed on the other side of the shower room. Steam wisped up from the bubbling water.

They keep that baby really hot.

I guess that's good for the swimmers to soothe their muscles after coming from the cold pool.

It won't be good for *your* muscles today, Mary, I thought.

I moved quickly to the supply cabinet. One more important hurdle to cross. One more lap before I could head for the finish of the race.

Had someone locked the cabinet?

No. I pulled open the door and peered inside.

My eyes swept from the top shelf to the bottom. Ace bandages and other medical supplies on top. One shelf of gray towels. Books and papers and equipment manuals on the next shelf.

And at the bottom of the cabinet, my precious supplies. The things I needed to pay Mary back. To win Hope back.

The white plastic, gallon-size bottles of chlorine. I knelt down and counted six of them. Six gallons of chlorine.

That should be more than enough, I thought.

A few days before, I'd hidden by the lockers and watched the coach add chlorine to the Jacuzzi. She'd poured about two cups into the dispenser on the side. The chlorine would be fed into the circulating water a little at a time.

Six gallons will do the trick, I knew. I hoisted the first one off the floor. Heavier than I thought. But I dragged it over to the bubbling Jacuzzi, pulled off the cap—and poured the clear liquid into the steaming water.

I carefully replaced the empty gallon bottle on the floor of the cabinet and lifted out another one.

It took longer than I thought to pour all six gallons of chlorine into the Jacuzzi. I was just emptying the last bottle when I heard the door swing open and heard girls' voices from the hall.

I swung around quickly. Tossed the empty bottle into the cabinet. Shut the door.

Behind me, bare feet slapped the concrete floor. I heard a girl complain about how cold the pool was. A girl sneezed. Two girls called out, "Bless you."

I backed away from the Jacuzzi. Found the hiding place I'd picked out days ago—an empty cubby way in the back, where no one ever went.

In front of me, the Jacuzzi steamed and gurgled.

Holding my breath, I slipped into my dark hiding place.

And waited.

The girls changed quickly into their street clothes. Most of them seemed in a hurry to leave.

I heard someone call to Mary. "Are you coming to dinner?"

Mary moved into view. I saw her pull off her swim cap. Her red hair bounced out. She had her back to me. She adjusted her swimsuit. Then she raised one leg and rubbed her knee.

"Mary—you're always the last one dressed," one of her teammates said.

"I just want to go in the whirlpool for a few minutes," Mary replied. "My leg muscles are all cramped."

Voices trailed off down the hall. The training room door slammed shut.

A few seconds later, the room stood silent.

I peeked out from my dark corner and, between the rows of metal lockers, I could see Mary. She dropped a white towel beside the Jacuzzi. Then, resting a hand on the chrome ladder, she stepped into the steaming water.

I poked my head out farther. I wanted to see what happened next.

I watched her lower herself into the swirling, hot pool.

I could see her face and her pale shoulders above the water.

It took a few seconds before she started to scream.

Her mouth opened in shock. Her hands shot up.

Her shrill cry echoed off the walls and metal lockers.

"Ohhhhh! Help me! Somebody—*help!*"

She thrashed the water. She raised herself up but appeared to fall.

She screamed again. "It burns! Oh, help! It *burrrrrrns!*"

Her face flamed bright red now.

The water splashed and churned.

She pulled at her hair with both hands. "Help me! Somebody! I'm burning! I'm burning!"

Screaming, she lurched across the pool, sending a wave of water crashing over the side. She splashed and thrashed some more. Then I saw one hand grab the railing, and she pulled herself out.

Her eyes were wild. She held her head with both hands. And staggered over the floor.

Her skin—her arms, her legs—were red as fire.

Squinting through the lockers, I saw the skin on her arms start to peel.

"Help me! Help me!"

She dropped to her knees, still wailing and crying.

And someone appeared. A woman bent over Mary. The swim team coach. She tried to wrap a towel around Mary's shoulders.

"I'm burning! Make it stop burning!" Mary wailed.

The towel fell off. Blisters had formed on her shoulders.

The coach grabbed for the towel. "I don't know what to do!" she screamed.

"Help me! Help me!" Mary wailed, her cries growing weaker.

And then the coach turned, wide-eyed and open-mouthed. She turned—and stared right at me.

I'm caught, I realized.

I'm trapped back here. Nowhere to escape.

What do I do now?

FEAR STREET ®

R L STINE

SUPER CHILLER

- ☐ PARTY SUMMER — 72920-9/$3.99
- ☐ BROKEN HEARTS — 78609-1/$3.99
- ☐ THE DEAD LIFEGUARD — 86834-9/$3.99
- ☐ BAD MOONLIGHT — 89424-2/$3.99
- ☐ THE NEW YEAR'S PARTY — 89425-0/$3.99
- ☐ SILENT NIGHT — 73822-4/$3.99
- ☐ GOODNIGHT KISS — 73823-2/$3.99
- ☐ SILENT NIGHT 2 — 76619-9/$3.99
- ☐ CHEERLEADERS: THE NEW EVIL — 86835-7/$3.99
- ☐ GOODNIGHT KISS 2 — 52969-2/$3.99
- ☐ SILENT NIGHT 3 — 52970-6/$3.99
- ☐ HIGH TIDE — 52971-4/$3.99

FEAR HALL

- ☐ THE BEGINNING — 00874-9/$3.99

FEAR PARK

- ☐ #1: THE FIRST SCREAM — 52955-2/$3.99
- ☐ #2: THE LOUDEST SCREAM — 52956-0/$3.99
- ☐ #3: THE LAST SCREAM — 52957-9/$3.99

CATALUNA CHRONICLES

- ☐ THE EVIL MOON — 89433-1/$3.99
- ☐ THE DARK SECRET — 89434-X/$3.99
- ☐ THE DEADLY FIRE — 89435-8/$3.99

Available from Archway Paperbacks
Published by Pocket Books